Green

Year

1961

BY EVAN MACKRILL

1. *Furniture polish and potpurri*

Raindrops on car windows can be anything, worms wiggling across the glass, or racing cars chasing each other to the bottom, or perhaps musical notes crashing into each other to create new sounds, raindrops on car windows can be anything when you are a bored eight-year-old. Jean was small for her age; rosy cheeked and spent most of her time lost in her daydreams. Just as Jean's head fell heavy with sleep, the sharp sound of car wheels rolling over gravel shot her eyes open. They had arrived.

The car jolted to a halt. Jean's mother stepped out of the driver's door and moved hastily over to the handle of Jean's door, gracefully unravelling and wielding high an umbrella as she did so.

"Come on then Jean, lift those eye lids and heels."

Jean's mother was young, smart, stern and poised. She glared at Jean with striking blue eyes framed by a pair of large round glasses. Jean grabbed her mother's hand and wearily tottered alongside her. The car keys were placed in the palm of an elderly man, dressed in a regal green jacket and hat as he gestured for Jean and her mother to make their way across a courtyard, towards a set of stone stairs. The stairs lead to a teak brown monolithic set of doors. The shy crunch of gravel was replaced by the clack of hard heels on stone steps, a second elderly man with an identical green jacket opened the door, with a hospitable urgency he beckoned Jean and her mother into the building.

His mouth opened slowly to begin his over rehearsed lines:

"Welcome Ms Maple to Hills Bottom Manor. May I take your coat and umbrella and invite you to dry by the foyer fireplace, while Mrs Grey records you as having arrived."

He gave a nod to a sour faced woman behind an almost comically oversized desk.

With their wet clothes now placed on the back of an armchair in front of the fire both Jean and her mother grew two warm smiles together, this comfort did not last long as Mrs Grey appeared vulturic behind them.

"Ladies, please join me in walking to your room, your coats can remain here, I shall send Robert the doorman to deliver them to your room, after they have been allowed time to dry of course." Mrs Grey's tone was harsh, but reassuringly Jean felt that this was always her manner.

Hills Bottom Manor was grand, with sets of ostentatious staircases twisting through the walls. Paintings littered the richly wallpapered walls and intricate floral patterns framed the ceilings, the smell of furniture polish and potpurri added to the grand atmosphere.

Jean's legs were tired of climbing stairs, something both her mother and Mrs Grey could sense, but the pair continued at the same pace none the less. Jean caught up to them as they arrived at room 49, which was discretely labelled by the presence of a small gold engraved plaque mounted low on the wall. For a moment Jean stared at her own warped and rosy reflection in the plaque's glossy finish.

Mrs Grey and Jean's mother began to talk in the centre of the room; Jean ignored their conversation and lazily made her way to the one large window. The rain rapped against the glass fiercely and loudly.

"Wales is wet", she sighed.

2. *Blotting*

After settling into their room, changing into dry clothes and navigating their way downwards through the maze of hallways and stair sets, Jean and her mother nestled themselves opposite each other hugged within two large, stiff, worn, moat green reading chairs within a dark corner of a lounge area of the manor, directly opposite the entrance hallway. Her mother had gathered a brick thick pile of the day's newspapers and had begun reading every word at a furious pace, her glasses exaggerating the mad flickering of her eyes.

Ripples in fabric can be anything, they can be waves for imaginary boats, or desert sand dunes, or even the bark texture from a giant oak trunk, ripples in fabric can be anything when you are a bored eight-year-old. Jean was pitching and reshaping the creases and wrinkles in her deep navy swing dress, she was attempting to become lost in her daydreams, but her self-awareness of her boredom prevented her mind wondering too far into her own thoughts. Her eyes begun to drift around the room, they fixed upon a set of eyes staring back at her from the opposite corner, the set of eyes belonged to a wiry, drawn, sharp nosed, scowling elderly woman in a long grey dress and matching jacket, with a deep green scarf wrapped tightly around her long neck. Jean thought that she looked like a witch. The two of them had now shared a gaze for too long, Jean felt it now necessary to walk over and introduce herself, she sheepishly slid from the armchair and walked with hesitance across the dimly lit lounge, the witchy woman's eyes remained fixed to her. Jean was now close enough to see the depth of her wrinkled and distinct cheek bones, which seemingly tried to escape from her pale grey skin. Jean stood formally in front of the writing desk that the staring woman was sat behind.

"Good evening, my name is Jean Maple, I am eight years old, it's a pleasure to meet you." Jean said exactly as her mother had made her rehearse.

The woman behind the desk paused, rolled her eyes and raised one edge of her mouth to form a displeasured snarl-like grimace, her pause lasted for an oddly long time before she responded.

"I am Mrs Moss, Miss Maple have you ever heard the common saying: Children should be seen and not heard?" Mrs Moss harshly questioned with a raspy Welsh accent.

Jean's expression was a confused one.

"It is very nice to meet you Mrs Moss, I have not heard of your saying before."

Mrs Moss replied, "I am not surprised."

During the pairs conversation Mrs Moss had coiled her twiggy grey fingers around a thick black fountain pen and had started tapping it uncontrollably on the small piece of note paper, placed in the centre of the writing desk in front of her. Ink flow dripped from the silver tip on the page until the ink created black pools on the paper. Jean noticed the tapping; she focused on it briefly but decided not to bring it to Mrs Moss's attention and instead continued to ask Mrs Moss questions to suppress her boredom.

"Mrs Moss, may I ask what you are writing?"

Mrs Moss responded immediately with a sharp tone:

"You mean to say, what was I writing, before you interrupted." She sighed, twitched her gaze from jean and instead stared into the flames of the fireplace, which dimly illuminated the room from the centre of the wall between Jean's mother and the writing desk. Mrs Moss continued, "But, I suppose if you must know, I am writing Christmas letters."

Just as abruptly as Mrs Moss had answered Jean responded likewise:

"Christmas letters, It is January!"

The frequency of the tapping of the fountain pen on the desk increased.

"You are rather small for an eight-year-old." Snapped Mrs Moss, she glared back at Jean.

Jean was taken a back, her eyebrows raised themselves and her cheeks flushed pink.

"Maybe I am small, but you are old and mean!"

The pen tapping on the desk may as well have been a dagger in the beak of a woodpecker. They both firmly clenched their mouths closed for a few seconds, but unavoidably Jean's attention was drawn back to the uncontrolled and furious tapping, the pen tip had now scratched through the soggy black paper, the ink was pooling within the wood grain of the desk, bleeding across the surface. Jean was not the only person who had become fixated by the repetitive tapping sound; Robert, the doorman who had greeted Jean and her mother into the Manor earlier that afternoon stood in the doorway of the lounge, his eyes fixated on the pen. Robert shuffled over to the writing desk with a calming smile and a now relaxed demeanour. He simply nodded to Jean and extended his hand out for Jean to grasp, Jean obliged to this gesture and let Robert walk her slowly back across the room to the dark corner where her mother still sat. Robert turned his neck to look back at Mrs Moss.

"You can stop blotting your pen now Mrs Moss." Robert softly suggested.

Mrs Moss's brow was still fixed as a frown, but her furious pen tapping slowed to an eventual halt.

Once returned to the two opposing armchairs Robert knelt beside Jean, their eyes level.

"It might be wise to avoid Mrs Moss, instead of talking to her would you prefer a warm glass of milk?" Robert's voice was soft; the softness was exaggerated by his subtle Welsh accent and elderly tone. Jean's mother looked up from her papers and slowly rose the corners of her mouth to signify that the warm milk was approved.

Robert continued to hold Jean's hand and led her out of the lounge, they walked past the entrance desk where Mrs Grey stood looming over all like a judge, nose firmly pointed skywards. Jean felt that her presence within the manor was an annoyance to Mrs Grey, owing to her disposition. Despite Mrs Grey's eyes tracking the pair as they walked across the entrance hall her gargoyle expression and statuesque stance did not change.

Jean and Robert turned right through an arched doorway perpendicular to the entrance hallway, which led them into a tunnel like corridor with a set of double doors at its end, Jean and Robert continued. Robert gave one of the doors a firm push which flung the door dramatically open.

The noise that hit Jean's eardrums was anarchic, the smells that shot into her nostrils were striking and the heat of this new room felt like a wave crashing over her, they had entered the Kitchen of Hill's Bottom Manor. The kitchen was lively to say the least, bells were ringing, cabinet doors were slamming, glasses were clinking, pans were clattering and just like Crows in the trees the various members of kitchen staff squawked over one another. Steam created a dense uncomfortable air. Jean had experienced nothing like this before and stood overwhelmed. The steam parted to reveal a tall imposing woman, who somehow appeared even more imposing than Mrs Grey, due to her height, wide shoulders, scarlet forehead and the two large knifes clenched white knuckle tight in each fist, she wore a white collared dress and a large moss green apron that almost made it to the tops of her knees.

"Good evening Cook, one warm cup of milk for the young Miss Maple please." Robert said politely.

The lady addressed as "Cook" replied with an impassive single nod, turned her back and paced rapidly back into the steam. She immerged implausibly seconds later with a tumbler glass half full of milk, she extended it towards Jean, Jean reached up and with two hands held the tepid glass.

"Thank you Cook." Robert said as he placed his hand on Jean shoulder to turn her towards the double doors, the pair walk back through the double doors and into the corridor, leaving Cook to stare at them as say left.

"Kitchens are exciting places aren't they Miss Maple?" Robert asked with a rhetorical tone, he continued.

"We can go back there if you are ever bored and what to see it again"

Jean did not enjoy the experience of the loud Kitchen and thought to herself that it would be unlikely that she would ever want to go back, but she did enjoy the milk.

Robert guided Jean back to the armchair opposite her mother, all while under the watchful scrutiny of Mrs Grey behind her oversized desk. Jean sat bored, once again, as Robert shuffled to attend to other duties elsewhere. Whilst her mother was still reading through the day's papers Jean began to look around the lounge. Mrs Moss had left during Jean's milk excursion so there were no staring eyes to halt Jean's wandering gaze. There was a small square table in the corner with wooden chess pieces placed on top of it, Jean had seen chess pieces before but only pictures never in real life, she made a mental note to inspect them later. There were also two men that filled both window seats that faced the driveway of the manor; the seats were far enough apart to suggest that the men were not acquaintances. Both chairs faced the windows directly, Jean was only able to see the tops of their heads poking out from behind their armchairs. One man had night black hair; the other wore a bowler hat.

Jean was startled. A hand rested on hers.

"Come on Jean, supper." The hand was her mothers, she quickly grabbed Jean's wrist and pulled her from the chair, Jean's wondering thoughts were still with the two men in the window seats, before she knew it she was sat at a table with a steaming bowl of tomato soup and a torn shard of white bread on a saucer beside it. The smell of the soup was delightful to Jean, while her mother silently sat opposite her at the table, Jean ate and Jean thought back over the day's affairs, she thought about the rain, she thought about the chess pieces, she thought about Robert and Cook and Mrs Grey, she thought about bread and soup, and then, once again her mind shifted into the realisation of how tired she had become.

Fifteen minutes or so flashed by in a daze for Jean, who had sleepily eaten the remaining soup and had been guided by her mother up the stair set to room 49, she sat both half awake and half asleep on the edge of her bed. The bed was positioned beside a radiator, and on the opposite side of the room from her mother's. As she moved to lie down, she peered out of the room's window, the lights from the manor beamed out across the fields in front of them, the illumination from the light stopped as it met a dense wall of fog. As Jean wondered what was beyond the fog, her eyes closed and instead of wondering she began dreaming.

3. *Nothing to cause concern*

Screams woke Jean from her sleep, ear piercing, echoing, petrifying, skin chilling screams. Jean shot from the bed, as did the hairs from her neck and arms.

Her mother was already by the door, she opened it, Jean followed. Jean's mother took one step down the nearest flight of stairs, looked down, grabbed the banister, gasped and brought her other hand to her mouth. Jean ran to the banister to peer over following her mother's dramatics. Below them a couple of flight of stairs down on a landing area led Mrs Moss, twisted, distorted with lifeless eyes staring back up at Jean. Her body was drained of the little colour it once had, a thick puddle of blood surrounded her, shards of bone had split through the skin of her legs and her limbs were fixed in unnatural contorted positions. She still wore her green scarf and grey dress and matching jacket, but her shoes were broken at the heels and rested a few stairs further down, her hair was matted and knotted with blood, still draining from the top of her head. A young female member of the Manor's staff disclosed by a green jacket she wore, that was almost identical to Robert's, was kneeling beside Mrs Moss white faced and hysterically wailing.

Mrs Grey and Robert ran onto the landing. Mrs Grey swooped in helping the distraught member of staff back to her feet and accompanying her into a nearby room. Robert threw a large dark green bed sheet over Mrs Moss as if she was a fire that needed suffocating. With Mrs Moss's motionless eyes now covered Jean felt that she could look away and grabbed the ruffles of her mother's dress. Jean had her eyes closed tight, but she could still see Mrs Moss's mangled corpse. Mrs Grey returned to the landing area, looking as fierce and as sour as always, Robert engaged her in a stern conversation, Jean and her mother were too far away to catch their words. Other guests had begun to creep out of their rooms, garbed in matching avocado dressing gowns, guests occupied most of the banister space overlooking Mrs Grey and Robert, the gallery seats were full for the night's show.

Mrs Grey shouted upwards into the spiral of stairs and guests above her:

"There has been an unfortunate accident, nothing to cause concern, please return to your rooms and if you have questions I shall address them in the morning, good night to all!"

No one replied directly to Mrs Grey, but there were more than a few guests that muttered sentences under their breath. Jean's mother did not speak; she placed her hands on Jean's shoulders and guided her back into room 49.

4. *We are most unwelcome*

Scrambled eggs on a plate can be anything, clouds floating across a plate sky, or sheep in a field, or perhaps tumbleweed rolling across the scene of a western film. Scrambled eggs on a plate can be anything when you are a bored eight-year-old. Jean sat opposite her mother at one of the breakfast tables in the restaurant room of the Manor, her mother again nose deep into her habitual reading of the day's newspapers. Jean may have been bored but her mine was fall of thoughts, the image of Mrs Moss's mangle body haunted her, she had not slept since returning to the room and had instead stared at the walls and ceiling until her mother's alarm clock flickered into action.

Jean suddenly felt uneasy and looked around the room, the dozen or so guests eating breakfast at other tables had all downed tools, widened their eyes and turned their heads to face the entrance of the room. Where through the lens of an archway well positioned dining room guests were able to make out the baronial entrance door to the Manor and a corner of the reception desk. Jean was well placed for viewing and mimicked the actions of the other guests.

Two policemen entered the Manor. The pair were both round faced, dressed in full police uniform and black leather gloves, they promptly withdrew small black notebooks and pens from the lapel pockets of their jackets. Mrs Grey and Robert moved to stand directly in front of them. Jean was just able to overhear their conversation.

"Good morning, I am Inspector Lewis and this is Sergeant Lloyd."

"I am Mrs Grey and this is Robert, who is one of the doormen."

With introductions completed the two policemen seemed eager to dictate conversation; Inspector Lewis continued to speak in his strong Welsh accent:

"We shall begin with a tour of the house and grounds, if you would be so kind to guide us Mrs Grey, and if Robert would be so kind to take our bags to our rooms that would be hugely appreciated."

"Bags?" Mrs Grey sharply interrupted.

Unstartled Inspector Lewis continued: "We shall be staying the night as a matter of precaution Mrs Grey."

Robert had begun to shuffle out of the entrance door, presumably to collect the officer's bags from their car.

With an uncharacteristic flutter in her voice Mrs Grey said: "We are not expecting two more guests, I do not think that an elderly lady falling downstairs requires officers to stay an evening."

"Well, it seems that we are most unwelcome, odd." Sergeant Lloyd began to write within his black notebook.

Mrs Grey's eyes were fixed to the pen's movements. "Although I do not believe it is required, you are in luck, as we have two single rooms left vacant this evening."

Robert re-entered with two black duffle bags.

Mrs Grey continued. "Robert shall take your bags to the single rooms, I shall show you to your rooms at the end of our Hills Bottom Manor tour." She gave an obviously forced smile to both Officers.

The four of them walked off down the entrance corridor, out of Jean's sight.

Jean looked blankly into her cold scrambled eggs.

5. *Darruwala*

After what seemed like an eternity to Jean her mother had finished reading every story in the paper, she stood up and grabbed Jean by the hand to lead her to their room. Their route past the reception desk was now obscured by a line of guests which had formed during their meal. Mrs Grey stood behind the desk barrier, ready for confrontation. A tall, elegant lady dressed head to toe in teal stood at the front of the queue.

"Mrs Grey I find your lack of understanding most alarming." said the Teal Lady.

"I simply cannot refund rooms based on another guest accidentally falling down stairs, you may leave whenever you like but the nights room that you have paid for is not refundable." Replied Mrs Grey, she extended out a rigid open palm to the Teal Lady.

The Teal Lady was holding a room key within her right hand, upon Mrs Grey extending out an arm the teal lady withdrew her hand close to her chest, dishearten and beaten the Teal Lady turned her nose up at Mrs Grey, swivelled around and paced away towards the stairs with her teal heels cracking crisply against the hard floor of the entrance corridor. Others in the queue murmured amongst themselves, but none seemed brave enough to take on Mrs Grey. Jean rarely started conversations but at this moment so many thoughts were running through her mind that she ignored the fact that others were in the room and blurted out:

"Mother, did Mrs Moss fall?" The muttering stopped and the room fell silent, with the queue of guests eager to hear the answer. Jean's mother looked intensely at each of the guests, and then at Jean, she feigned a smile.

"Well, there was a lot of blood." she calmly said

Having now deserted her post victorious Mrs Grey was on her way through the entrance archway into the dining room, without turning to view the intended receivers of her statement she interjected: "There are a lot of steps to fall down."

Jean's expression was a confused one, she did not entirely understand the statement from either her mother or Mrs Grey. The guests dispersed into other rooms, and with a now tighter grip Jean's mother guided her up the many stairs towards room 49.

Once they were back within the familiar cosy comfort of their room Jean's mother began to silently hand Jean clothes from the dark wood wardrobe, a light blue floral brocade dress, a matching jacket, a white Alice band, white frilled socks, Jean's most comfortable shoes and an oversized bell-shaped beige anorak.

Once dressed Jean and her mother made for the Manor's front door, they both gave a Doorman a friendly nod as they left to sit on the welcoming leather seats of an awaiting taxi. Whilst moving Jean's eyes were fixed to the window, she was hoping to see something overwhelmingly exciting that she could hold with her in the no doubt boring times to come. The journey was short, Jean had no luck with discovering excitement through the window. The taxi stopped, Jean climbed out and slammed the heavy car door and waited for her mother to meet her. Jean's face was blank, her mother sensed her confusion.

"We have come to Hill's Bottom Jean, to look around and I need a new notebook." Explained her mother.

Jean smiled, as an eight-year-old she enjoyed exploring very much. The village of Hill's Bottom was framed with green hills and fields of livestock; it consisted of one long street, which ran parallel to a wide but shallow river, all the homes and local shops were positioned on just one side of the road, with the river opposite.

Her mother led Jean into many grey stone buildings with wooden window fronts, Jean loved everything about the stores, she loved the chiming ring of the entrance bells, she loved the hand painted embellished fonts that made up store front windows, signs and displays, she loved glass cabinets and she loved the cosy feeling of being surrounded by new items. Jean's visit to each shop was fleeting, her mother was pacing around, but eventually they stalled within a stationary store. Jean's mother was welcomed by the shop owner, a large red-faced lady with a floral blouse and vapid expression, the two engaged in friendly small talk but Jean continued into the shop to explore. She came across a shelf of fountain pens, they looked majestic with metallic tips and accents that could have blended seamlessly into a jewellery cabinet, and deep regal coloured packaging provided an interesting contrast to the shine of the metal. Jean picked up a gold tipped pen with a dark green barrel, the tip was long and elegant, she began to push the tip into the end of her thumb, she wondered if this pen would have survived under the ownership of Mrs Moss. She thought back to Mrs Moss at the bottom of the stairs and remembered her lifeless eyes. Jean removed the fountain pen tip from the end of her thumb and placed it back within its accompanying dark green open case. She moved on to the adjacent shelf, notebooks. While looking across the shelf one notebook drew Jean's hand to it, it was a plain black notebook. Jean picked the book up and flipped open the cover to examine the blank pages.

Jean's mother placed her hands on Jean's shoulders, she reached down and took the black notebook from Jean's grip.

"This one shall be perfectly fine, thank you Jean." Said her mother

She handed the book to the shop owner, who had now positioned herself behind a desk at the back wall of the shop. Money was handed over before Jean's Mother guided her outside, the black taxi was parked tight to the pavement. The pair slid back into the taxi, and Jean was back to searching for excitement through the lens of the taxi window.

The sky began to grey, rain fell hard, whatever excitement was outside the window for Jean was now masked in a watery blur. Today Jean was a little too tired to imagine raindrops as race cars, and so she looked away from the window, she rubbed her hand back and forth across the black leather of the taxi seats.

"Father would have liked this Taxi." said Jean softly, she was shocked that she accidently let her thoughts slip out as sound; she felt a hot flush rush from her heart to her face.

"Jean!" Her mother said shortly, sharply and through clenched teeth, her tone was as fierce as Mrs Moss's had been.

Jean's eyes shot to her shoes, her mother had given Jean one rule during their trip away:

Do not mention your father.

Jean's contemplation remained fixed at her shoes for the rest of the journey back to the manor, even until Jean and her mother sat opposite each other once again in the dark green lounge armchairs, but as Jean realised that her mother's attention was occupied with her newly purchased black notebook her head lifted, and she turned her neck to look around the lounge. The chess set on the small square table in the corner deserved more investigating today, she timidly walked across the room and sat on the stall at one vertices of the wooden table. All pieces seemed purposefully placed, all except one, Jean did not know the names of each piece or what they meant but one of the smallest pieces was laying horizontally, she picked it up from the chequered board and brought it close to one eye. She assessed every grain line and with her fingertips felt each curve, she thought that it was a beautifully shaped item and wondered what purpose each curve had and what they signified. She placed the piece as it was, horizontal and out of the regimented lines of the others, maybe this one piece was meant to be placed differently from the rest, she thought, even though it did not feel right to her and from memory she believed them to all be within rows the previous evening. Without picking up the other pieces Jean moved her head closer to them for closer inspections. Jean shifted her focus from looking at the pieces to looking through the regimented lines of wooden ornaments. She saw a set of eyes staring back at her from across the room, the set of eyes belonged to a vibrant character that was sat at Mrs Moss's writing desk.

This staring figure was an elderly man, a man who Jean felt sure was the owner of the night black hair that she saw before, poking out from the top of the window seat chairs. This man was fascinating to Jean; he was unlike any other man she had ever seen. As their stares met Jean felt obliged to walk over to speak to him, Jean gawked and walked, she had already thought of many questions for this peculiar man.

"Do you like Chess?" the man questioned.

"How has your skin become so brown?" Jean paid no attention to the man's question.

The man was briefly taken a back, but then laughed softly. "Because of that question I assume that you have never seen anyone like me before."

"I certainly have not Mr." Jean responded, she was also taken a back, the man's accent was as peculiar to Jean as his look, it was like nothing she had ever heard before, every word rolled and sounded warm.

"Mr, May I also ask why you speak like that?" Jean continued to question.

The man laughed again. "To answer both of your questions, I have always had skin this colour, and although my accent has changed a little with time, I speak like this because I am from India and so have an Indian accent. I am Mr Patel."

"P-AH-TELL." Jean sounded out the word.

Mr Patel felt that he should continue: "Well my name is not really Patel, but the British seem to warm to me so much quicker if I use the name Patel, so my name has been Patel for eight years."

Jean smiled wide and replied: "Eight is as old as I am." She was happy to notice a coincidence. "Your name is as old as I am. So your name is not a real name?"

"My real name is Darruwala, but people like Patel. May I ask what your name is?" Mr Patel asked

"My name is Jean Maple." Said Jean with a proud stance, her hands behind her back and a beaming smile across her rose red cheeks.

"Nice to meet you Jean Maple." Replied Mr Patel

Jean stared for a little too long at Mr Patel's brightly patterned oddly shaped shirt which he wore under a light brown tweed jacket. The patterns on the shirt were made from swirls, lines and simple plant like shapes, the patterns were a mix of fiery colours, Jean had never seen anything like it before. Mr Patel noticed her staring.

"You have not seen a shirt like this before, have you?" As he already knew the answer Mr Patel continued. "It is a shirt from Kenya, everyone sports these over there, I've grown quite fond, particularly because of the grey weather, I feel that Hill's Bottom could do with a little more colour at this time of year."

Jean enjoyed the colours and gave Mr Patel a reassuring simper, he gave a childlike grin back in return.

"Are you from Kenya?"

"Oh no no no, no," Mr Patel laughed softly again "I am from India, I am Indian."

Jean had heard of India before, but knew very little, she asked: "What is India like Mr Patel?"

"Well, I shall show you" Mr Patel opened a large green leather backed book, the first page was full of small pencil sketches of plants. "These are some plants that you can find in India."

"One moment." Jean interrupted. Jean walked over to the stall by the square Chess table and dragged it across the room to position it next to Mr Patel's chair behind the writing desk. The loud shuddering sound of the stall being dragged across the wooden floor prompted Jean's Mother to let out a sharp and violent "Shhh!" Jean ignored her mother's noise and perched herself on to the stall beside Mr Patel.

Mr Patel continued to slowly turn the pages of his sketchbook and described the contents as he went, he first showed Jean a few pages of plants, which led into being a few pages of buildings, then a few pages of animals, then a few pages of people, then fruits, vegetables and spices, then market scenes, then water scenes, a few sketches of rooms. Then Mr Patel flicked to a page which had one word-like mark in the centre of it: 'આફ્રિકા' This was completely alien to Jean.

Mr Patel stopped at this page and turned to Jean. "Would you now like to see what Africa looks like?"

"Yes please Mr Patel, did you draw all of these things?"

"Yes I did, before I retired my job was to draw pictures for Newspapers, I used to practise by drawing everything I saw, you can never predict what will be in the News, so I practised drawing everything." Mr Patel gave Jean another one of his endearing childlike grins, as he turned the 'આફ્રિકા ' page of

his book to reveal more sketches of plants.

Jean focused on every detail of the sketches, she did not pay attention to Mr Patel's commentary as he described each sketch, but she loved to see the sketches up close, it was as if she was there, with each sketch being both exceptionally realistic and detailed.

"Mr Patel!" A voice shouted.

Startled the pair both quickly raised their heads and looked across the room, Sergeant Lloyd and Inspector Lewis stood in the arched entrance way between the lounge and the entrance corridor.

"Please excuse me Miss Maple, it seems as if I am being summoned." Said Mr Patel as he slid his chair back and grabbed a dark wooden cane resting on the arm of his chair. He slowly made his way across the lounge, scuffling his slippers across the dark wooden floor.

He stood in the archway to the room facing the pair of policemen, his expression begun as peaceful as Jean had always seen it, but slowly as the conversation continued his eyebrows came down, the wrinkles on his forehead grew deeper, the corners of his mouth dropped, and his eyelids started to narrow. Jean could not make out the words of the conversation, as their voices were lowered, but due to Mr Patel's change in expression she felt as though it would not be well received if she was to move closer into eavesdropping range. She instead tried to distract herself with the many sketches within Mr Patel's book. Jean tried to imagine the smells of each flower and the colours their petals would be, what noises the animals would make and the life stories of the people Mr Patel had sketched. Unfortunately, even the most detailed of Mr Patel's drawings could not stop Jean from looking towards the two policemen and Mr Patel, she remembered why they were here, she remembered Mrs Moss's twisted broken limbs.

Enough time had now past for Jean to feel slightly uneasy about sitting behind the writing desk on her own, although she had been flicking over the pages, she had not looked at a page of Mr Patel's book for a while. She wondered if Mr Patel would be able to return at all and felt that it would now be perfectly acceptable if she were to leave the desk and return to the armchair to re-join her mother. Jean closed the book, slid from her stool and quietly walked back over to the tall dark green worn armchairs.

Jean's mother gave her a sharp look, as if to say, 'do behave Jean', she then returned her gaze to her new black notebook. The armchair that Jean sat in was well placed to see one half of the reception desk, Mrs Grey poised behind it, her grey hair scratched back into a bun and her thin lips shut tight and perfectly horizontal. There was a rap of heels on the hallway floor, the owner of the heels was the Teal lady who was dressed in the same attire as she was during the morning, she abruptly stopped once she reached the reception desk, turned to face Mrs Grey, extended her right arm violently and dropped a set of keys on to the desk, Mrs Grey and the Teal lady exchanged a few short words that Jean could not make out, and with bag in hand and Robert in pursuit the Teal lady made for the exit, Jean briefly heard the howl of the wind, then the door slammed.

With her armchair being slightly closer than the stool behind the writing desk to the lounge entrance Jean could now take a closer look at both Inspector Lewis and Sergeant Lloyd, although she still could not hear them. The two police officers looked remarkably similar, especially as both were in uniform, they were fairly tall with wide frames and round faces, the only defining features were the short black beard and the larger eyebrows of Inspector Lewis, the pair's expressions now matched Mr Patel's, disgruntled and angry.

Jean became bored of being unable to hear them and began to think again of Mr Patel's sketches.

"Mother!"

Jean's cry caught her mother's attention; she looked up from her notebook and gave Jean a coy smile.

"May I borrow one of your pens and a page from your book?" Jean questioned.

Her mother lent over to her handbag by the side of her armchair and picked out a silver ball point pen, she silently handed it to Jean. Once she had the pen in hand her mother tore a single page out of the very back of her black notebook and offered it to Jean. She took the pen and gave her mother an appreciative smile.

Jean slid from the armchair and quickly walked over to the writing desk, sitting back on her stool she placed the notebook page in front of her and beside Mr Patel's large book. For a moment the lines of the page stared inertly back at Jean as she contemplated what to draw, she searched around the room for inspiration and quickly realised the same figure sat with a bowler hat on one of the window seats of the lounge. From the new angle of the writing desk Jean could see a little more of the figure. Sat on the window seat was a man wearing formal trousers, a white suit shirt, bright red braces and a bowler hat. The red braces and bowler hat made him appear clown-like to Jean, in an endearing way. Jean begun to sketch him. She started with a large arcing line to represent the top of the bowler hat, she then circled it to create the brim, a small semi-circle underneath it for his face, two small dots for his eyes, a larger triangle for the protruding nose, a thin small line for his mouth, two large streaking rectangles beneath that for his pair of braces, and two triangles between them for his shirt collar.

"Miss Maple."

Jean jumped.

"Hello Miss Maple." Mr Patel repeated, "Sorry to startle you, I'm glad that my book has served to give you some aspiration to sketch for yourself, what are you drawing?" Mr Patel sat on the seat next to Jean's stool.

"I am drawing that man over there." Jean answered as she moved her head to nod in the direction of the window, where the bowler hatted man sat.

"Well in that case I shall join you." Brushing open his tweet jacket to reveal more of his vibrant shirt Mr Patel withdrew a sharp pencil from the scabbard that was his lining pocket, threw open his book to one of the last pages, which was morning snow pure, and peered thoughtfully at the bowler hatted man. Jean had abandoned her own sketch, with her attention now absorbed into watching Mr Patel's actions. After taking a still thoughtful moment of contemplation Mr Patel began to draw lines on the page, thin quick line some seeming soft and barely visible, some dark and deliberate and slowly but surely the side profile of the man with a bowler hat had appeared on the page. After a few impactful finishing strokes Mr Patel downed his pencil, lent back in his chair and looked down with accomplishment at his work. Jean looked up at him and blurted out the thought that sprung to her mind:

"I think we should show him Mr Patel, I feel that it may be rude to draw someone and then not show them, and he may love seeing it."

Mr Patel appeared to debate Jean's statement within his own thoughts, before delivering a cautious response:

"Yes I suppose that I agree, I have never thought of it as rude before, please show him his sketch, if you like." Mr Patel smiled, picked up his book and handed it over to Jean as she extended out her arms.

Jean carefully edged off the stool and gingerly made her way across the wooden floor to the window seats.

In between the two armchairs that faced the twinned windows there was a low circular dark wood side table. Place neatly on the table were half a dozen piles of differently sized paper, seemingly belonging to the bowler hatted man, Jean placed the open book on top of the smallest pile. The bowler hatted man lifted his head away from the handful of paper in his hands and peered over the piles to look down at Jean and Mr Patel's open book.

"What's this then?" questioned the bowler hatted man, in a high and faintly Welsh voice.

"Why it is a drawing of you, can you tell?" Jean said with a large grin across her face.

"May I take a closer look" The bowler hatted man extended out an open hand towards Jean.

Jean obliged, she picked the book up off the smallest pile of papers and placed it in the man's palm, he grabbed it from her, he held in in one hand with his thumb in the crease.

"Yep, that's me for sure, did you draw this, or perhaps your mother?" As he asked this his mouth grew wide across his wide face and stopped once it had created a devilish smirk.

Jean laughed slightly. "no, no I am only eight years old and my mother, actually, I have never seen my mother drawing anything" She paused for second and watched the man's smile fall limp.

"But, but this drawing was sketched by Mr Patel, over there just now." Jean said proudly as she flicked her hand over to gesture at both the writing desk and Mr Patel behind it.

The bowler hatted man did not move his eyes or head, he avoided following Jean's gesture and instead gave Jean a forced smile.

"Great it's a good drawing." The bowler hatted man said bluntly as he extended his arm out once again at Jean for her to take the book back.

Jean was somewhat disappointed and confused that the man had not taken a longer look at Mr Patel's book, but nonetheless she still softly grasped the book and brought it back into her possession.

Although her aim of showing the bowler hatted man the sketch of himself was completed Jean did not feel content at their interaction, and so decided to continue the conversation moving it in a different direction.

"I am Miss Jean Maple; may I ask what your name is?" Jean stood proudly, upright, with her chin lifted and her hands holding the sketchbook locked loosely behind her back.

"My name is Mr Paul Shean, how do you do." Mr Shean once again extended his arm out, but this time he was offering a handshake. Jean slightly apprehensively shook his hand, gave him an awkward look and continued her questioning:

"How do you do Mr Shean, may I ask why you have so many papers?"

Mr Shean smiled at the question, he gave a smile as if he was delighted to have caught a mouse in a trap, he removed his bowler hat to reveal a few thin brown curls of hair on the sides of his head and placed the hat beside him on the arm of his chair.

While still beaming he answered Jean's question excitedly without pausing for breath:

"I have many leaflets because I have many Televisions to sell to many people to educate many dreams to sell many pictures to show many hotels stores manors homes castles boats towers churches pavilions to fill with screens showing the imagination of the world's greatest minds." He abruptly stopped and looked at Jean.

Jean was taken a back and took some time to piece together the long collection of words Mr Shean had just bombarded her with.

"So these are leaflets with Televisions on them?" she said uneasily

"Only the Best televisions for all purposes all sizes for all rooms, do you own a television?" Jean started to shake her head, but Mr Shean gave her no time to answer and briskly continued. "Televisions are the future, imagine hotels with screens in every room and placed within hallways and lounges to entertain the guests what a fantastically, enthralling, lively hotel that would be wouldn't you agree?" He once again gave no pause for an answer. "Television shows would certainly be a welcome moment of joy for guests that have just seen the body of a murdered woman wouldn't you agree?"

"Murdered?" Jean loudly interrupted.

Mr Shean's smile fell to a more serious expression, his voice lowered, and his pace of speech relaxed.

"Well, I believe so, Mrs Moss was old but very stable on her feet, to me she was a horrible boring woman who met a horrible end, but a delightfully entertaining end for others, maybe someone thought that would be quite a fitting end for her."

Jean had not thought about death too much during her eight years and could not shift the image of Mrs Moss's contorted body to fully comprehend the macabre view of Mr Shean. Jean just stared blankly back at Mr Shean.

"Anyway, televisions are the future, just look at the joy they bring." As he said this, brushing the topic of Mrs Moss aside, he picked up a crisp brightly coloured leaflet and handed it to Jean.

Jean took it hesitantly and began to examine, the leaflet had a painted picture of a family sat closely around a television set, the glow from the screen illuminating the smiling faces.

"Do most families have a television in Wales?" Jean questioned.

"Well, all the best families do, and it's my job to show the other families what they are missing out on, does your family own a television set Miss Jean?"

"We do not, are they not expensive?" Jean recalled a moment a few months ago where her mother had taken her on a shopping trip, Jean had paused briefly to watch a suited man on a television set within a shop window, Jean's mother had sternly looked back at Jean and sharply said "They are expensive".

Mr Shean was poised ready to unleash his obviously prepared response. "They are reducing in price every year, as well as becoming more reliable and with better sound and picture quality, there has never been a better time to buy one."

Jean did not reply, instead she drifted into a daydream. A daydream where she pictured herself and her mother walking into the store with a television in the shop window, she watched as her mother handed over notes to the sales assistant behind the register in exchange for a large Television sized box.

Mr Shean took advantage of Jean's silence to continue his pitch. "Imagine being able to choose from an array of exciting shows, you would simply never be bored, imagine a television in this room now, you could watch anything."

Jeans eyes lit up at the thought of not being bored ever again.

"Could you put a Television in this room Mr Shean, please?" She took an excited step closer to Mr Shean, who recoiled back uncomfortably in this armchair, maintaining his distance from Jean.

"I would love nothing more to, but I cannot convince Mrs Grey to let me, and she is in charge around here." Mr Shean smirked.

"Why?" Jean quickly questioned

"Maybe she is just a mean person." Mrs Shean smirk grew with smugness.

"Well, my mother might be able to change her mind." Jean marched off abruptly, leaving behind Mr Shean and his smug smirk.

Jean's march took her to the side of her mother's tall green armchair, she placed her hand on her mother's knee to take her attention away from her black notebook.

"Mother. Do you think that this hotel lounge would be better with a television?"

Her Mother responded quickly to Jeans questions:

"No, I do not believe so, there are many guests reading papers, and many guests reading books, I am sure that these guests would find a television set an unwelcome distraction. Besides, there is nothing on television that you cannot read within a book or a newspaper."

Jean looked back blankly at her mother whilst she deliberated her mother's points. Whilst she felt compelled to agree with her mother, she also felt that watching a television show would be entertaining, and she was certainly sure that it would have been more entertaining than sitting on the tall green armchair opposite her mother for hours on end. Jean's train of thought then took her back to the sketches of Mr Patel, she imagined his sketches moving around a television screen. She then turned to face Mr Patel, he was slowly tucking his chair in behind the writing desk, the bright oranges of his shirt pattern danced with the orange glow of the fireplace.

As Mr Patel walked past Jean on the way out of the lounge, he lowered his head to whisper at Jean.

"It is time for my dinner." He happily said softly, Jean smiled back at him and returned his sketchbook to him with an outstretched arm.

Jean turned her head to face her mother; her eyes met her mother's inquisitive eyes below a scowling brow and behind her round frame glasses, which exaggerated her disapproving stare.

"What was in his book Jean?" Her mother pried

"Sketches, pencil drawings, of flowers, people, places, he is a drawer." Jean explained.

"Well, I guess anybody can learn how to draw, has he drawn Hill's bottom manor and the people within it?" She continued to question Jean

"Yes, I watched him draw that man over there by the window."

"He must have a keen interest in people and their appearances." Her mother sharply replied.

Jean once again stared blankly back at her mother whilst she tried to understand her mother's abrasive response.

6. *Without the accessory of knives*

Floral patterning on dining hall carpets can be anything, a winding track for an imaginary train, the blueprints of an intricate maze, or perhaps fantasy creatures from another world, floral patterning on dining hall carpets can be anything when you are a bored eight-year-old. Jean was slumped sideways across one of the arms of her dining chair, her head was drooped and facing the carpet. The carpet was a combination of greens and a mustard yellow, which together formed a detailed floral pattern. The carpet ran through the entirety of the sizable dining hall and only changed to become stone flooring at the archway connecting the dining hall to the entrance corridor. Jean and her mother sat at a different table to the one they dined on during breakfast that morning, this night they were at the opposite end. Jean no longer had the entertaining view of the Manor entrance; the other diners were her only visual distraction. Her mother was once again occupied reading, this time it was a fiction book, one with a drab picture-less cover, so Jean had little interest in asking her mother about the plot, she instead began to look around at the other guests.

The dining hall was made up of eleven tables, Jean had counted them but only three were occupied, her own table, a table where the two policemen sat, Inspector Lewis and

Sergeant Lloyd, and a final table which was most interesting to Jean as it housed a guest that she had not seen before. Sat on her own in the table furthest from the entrance and tucked in a corner was an elderly lady. Although she had chosen the most secluded of tables, she was difficult to ignore, she wore white frilled gloves with rings worn over the top, a cropped, collard, dark green jacket over a dog tooth fitted dress, and several large pearl necklaces with accompanying pearl earrings. She sat tall and confident picking up small pieces of food from her plate that balanced precariously on the end of her fork before disappearing between her crimson lips.

Jean had stared for too long, the elderly lady met her gaze, Jean quickly dropped her head down to once again face the carpet.

Soon after she heard long striding footsteps approaching. The strong thudding strides of Cook swiftly moved past. Cook was dressed as before with her white collard dress and green apron and seemed as lofty as Jean remembered, but this time without the accessory of knives. Jean thought back to when she had been at school, as Cook's pacey stride reminded her of an angry teacher marching across a hallway towards a troublesome pupil. Cook pulled an unused chair out from under the elderly lady's table and sat beside her, this was not to the liking of the elderly lady, Jean deduced this from her scowling expression.

The pair then began a heated argument but with all words as a hushed sharp whisper, both with gritted teeth. To Jean their argument was nothing but hissing, she had no clue as to what was being said, but she was certainly intrigued. As she looked around it seems she was not the only intrigued guest within the dining hall, both Inspector Lewis and Sergeant Lloyd had downed their knives and forks and were sat calmingly staring at the table where Cook and the elderly woman sat. After a minute or two it appeared that their curiosity could be restrained no longer, the pair shuddered their dining chairs back across the carpet, withdrew their black notebook from their pocket sheath and headed towards the elderly lady's table. Her argument with Cook abruptly ended.

Once tableside Inspector Lewis began to speak: "Good evening, Mrs Corsewell, I think it is about time that we had a conversation with you about manor proceedings."

The elderly lady who had now been named as Mrs Corsewell gave the two policemen a large false smile and with her hand gestured for them to take the remaining two seats at the table. Cook took this as her cue to leave; she stood up and strode out in a similar pacey fashion to her entry.

"I have heard that your presence is upsetting the guests, it is important not to upset guests." Mrs Corsewell bitterly explained as the two officers took their seats.

"Unfortunately, protocols must be taken Mrs Corsewell." Inspector Lewis spoke blandly without emotion, which was a stark contrast to Mrs Corsewell's raspy and thick accented voice.

"What is best for the manor opposes the views of policemen, an old lady fell, old ladies fall, I am far more aware of that than you both, I'm sure you will agree."

Jean was slightly afraid of Mrs Corsewell, she felt uncomfortably close to her conversation with the police and so decided to continue to look directly down at her empty plate, but she continued to eavesdrop.

The policemen ignored Mrs Corsewell's angry statement and continued with their questioning:

"So how old do you think Mrs Moss was?" Sergeant Lloyd asked, himself and Mrs Corsewll went back and forth.

"Old enough to fall."

"Did you ever meet Mrs Moss?"

"I rarely meet with guests; I keep myself to myself and focus on other matters."

"Has an accident similar to this ever happened before?"

"On occasion guests have tripped and fallen, but nothing more than scratches to report."

"You appear angry, what are your feelings at the moment?"

"Yes, I am angry, I am angry that you have forced yourselves upon us and I am angry at Mrs Moss, for her carelessness is the root of this, distress."

Inspector Lewis continued as Sergeant Lloyd wrote notes calmly in his black notebook.

"Mrs Corsewell, when a person dies the police must ask questions and assess the scene."

"The police could do so during normal working hours and do so without scaring away guests."

"Mrs Corsewell, a considerable amount of your guests saw the lifeless body of Mrs Moss on the staircase, they have to be questioned." Inspector Lewis paused briefly but without a response from Mrs Corsewell he continued. "I must say that our first impression seemed to suggest that the deceased fell by accident, however myself and Sergeant Lloyd have been met with such distaste and hostility from all of your staff and guests that we can't help but feel that something untoward is going on at the manor, it is also odd that every individual that we have questioned seems to share the same level of distaste towards Mrs Moss." He looked piercingly into Mrs Corsewell's eyes, Sergeant Lloyd's pen rose from the page with anticipation of Mrs Corsewell's response.

Her cheeks and brow now flushed she slowly opened her shrivelled lips: "From what I hear Mrs Moss was not a pleasant woman, and brought it on herself."

"Brought what on herself madam?" Sergeant Lloyd quickly interjected; pitch raised.

"Brought the distaste of others upon herself, she fell officers, now may I retire to my room for the rest of the day?" Mrs Corsewell stood up.

"Good evening, Mrs Corsewell." Said inspector Lewis, as she pushed her chair in and walked off flustered.

Jean's eyes were still fixed to her plate as Mrs Corsewell strode past. Jean thought back to Cook's equally as pacey stride and remembered how much she disliked walking fast, she wondered if most adults walked this way, and whether she would walk with a similar pace once she had grown. Jean also wondered as to whether or not her mother had joined her in eavesdropping.

"Mother does that lady own the Manor?" she questioned.

"Well, it seems so Jean, she does not appear to be enjoying her position at this current moment in time though, does she?" Her mother asked somewhat rhetorically.

Jean nodded in confirmation and shared a smile with her mother.

"Jean, shall we each ask for a hot chocolate, and drink them within the lounge?" Her mother asked.

Jean's smile widened and her nodding increased, she loved hot chocolate and she enjoyed the lounge. Jean removed the white napkin from her lap and took her mother's hand, the pair walked across the patterned carpet towards the entrance corridor.

The entrance door opened.

A chilling breeze burst in with the accompaniment of a few brown leaves and the first elderly gentlemen who had taken the car keys from Jean's mother upon their arrival.

"I beg your pardon ladies, both the rain and wind have become most, dramatic, out there."

Jean looked up at her mother, who gave nothing in response to the gentlemen's words apart from a stern look in his direction.

The wind and rain thrashed against the lounge windows as Jean and her mother resumed their now regular position on the rich green leather armchairs.

7. *Peered into the deep darkness*

The leather cracks and grooves on the arms of a chair can be anything, a winding series of rivers for miniature boats to cruise along, the bark texture of an old large tree, or perhaps canyons on the surface of another planet for aliens to live in, the leather cracks and grooves on an arm of a chair can be anything when you are a bored eight-year-old.

Jean's mother had caught the eye of a member of manor staff, the same young lady who the pair had seen in hysterics at the scene of Mrs Moss's accident, her face still flushed of colour.

"Can I please ask for two mugs of hot chocolate?" Jean's mother asked

"Certainly" the young lady replied frankly. She quickly paced away.

Jean rolled off her chair with boredom and begun her ritual of exploring the lounge room, she walked over to the now empty window seats and peered out of the window, she pushed her nose against the chilled glass and peered into the deep darkness. Two lights sparked into life, accompanied by the rumbling noise of a car engine flicking into action; the lights illuminated the circular front lawn of the manor, and in the process startled two crows perched on the surrounding fence, they made their way into the upper branches of the tall looming tree that cascaded over the lawn. The Car was sleek, low and silver, it crunched the stones of the manor's driveway as it drove off, making way for the hills. Jean thought back to the leather grooves of the armchair and imagined the silver car driving over the back of the chair as it cruised out of sight.

A rain drop hit the window between jeans eyes with a sharp ping, a second followed, within a matter of moments the window was full of water drops moving their way to the bottom of the pane. A deep rumble of thunder shock both jean and the manor. Jean turned to see the comforting sight of her mother's round glasses rested upon the brim of a steamy mug of hot chocolate, her own steaming mug was placed on the small square side table between the two large green armchairs.

Jean and her mother sat facing each other, exchanging smiles from behind their mugs. Jean's eyelids suddenly felt heavy, as if they were being drawn down by the warm mug under her lip. Just as Jean took the last weary sip her mother's hands took the mug from her and placed it back on the side table.

"Bedtime Jean."

The pair gave a friendly nod to Mrs Grey at the entrance desk; the friendly gesture was not reciprocated, they began to climb the winding stairs. Jean was reminded off their tiring arrival assent, her legs where already asleep and where only pushed along by her desire for the fresh hotel sheets.

Her mother took off her shoes, Jean took one final look out the window across the wind battered moorland, and she was lost to sleep.

8. *We're not safe*

Shapes within thick morning fog can be anything, small ships genteelly sailing across a grassy sea, or gargoyle like creatures, or perhaps the ghostly hauntings of past sheep, shapes within thick morning fog can be anything when you are a bored eight-year-old.

Jean had been woken by the cackle of Crows and was now sat with her chin in her hands gazing out the window, waiting for her mother to re-enter the room from her long bath.

Still misty eyed, with morning daze, Jean's view from her window was wearily becoming a lighter shade of grey, bright cracks were opening within the overcast sky and the fog on the distant moorland was thinning.

Jean's mother immerged from the bathroom, with a cloud of thick warm steam creeping into the room behind her, Jean rubbed her eyes.

"Come on Jean, quickly." Her mother instructed while fiercely waving her hand in the direction of the bathroom.

Jean plodded across the room with heavy feet and into the mist, swinging the door closed loudly behind her. She took a look at the blurred reflection of herself within the bathroom mirror. Jean placed her elbows on the edge of the sink and forced her stomach onto the rim of the basin, she stretched out one arm to, just with a few fingertips, brush across the mirror creating two lines of clarity amongst the condensation. Jean stared back at her blue eyes, short brown bob of hair and pink cheeks. She picked up a purple floral scented square bar of soap and rubbed it into the palm of her left hand until a small foamy purple puddle had formed, she turned the tap on and placed her now cupped hand briefly underneath, she lowered her head and spread the purple mixture across her face. Once satisfied that all areas of her face had been scrubbed thoroughly, she began to rinse the soap off by splashing water down from her forehead.

"Jean!" Her mother yelled.

Jean was dawdling, she grabbed hold of a towel, slightly damp with condensation and rubbed her face into it.

Her mother pushed open the door.

"Do hurry Jean."

Jean rushed from the bathroom; her mother dressed her in a blink of an eye and briskly whisked her into the corridor outside of their room.

The sounds of stern voices and the clatter of many shoes on the stone floor of the entrance corridor could be heard up through the spinning staircases. After navigating down the manor's staircases they stood on the final step. A crowd of guests filled the entrance hallway, Jean's mother pulled Jean's arm towards two thin dining chairs that were placed next to the base of the stairs and off to one side, the pair took their viewing seats.

A smartly dressed short man, with slicked back blond hair stood in front of Mrs Grey at the reception desk, as if he was first inline of the most disorderly queue. He stood nose up and frowning, waving a newspaper under Mrs Grey's nose, a handful of the guests had newspapers aloft, but all had their luggage to hand. Jean could pick out a few scattered phrases amongst the congealed hum of the small crowd.

"We shall not stay a minute longer."

"We're not safe!"

"This is a crime scene!"

Jean's mother rose from her chair and gently rested her hand on the shoulder of the nearest lady within the crowd, the lady sharply swivelled around, Jean's mother gestured to the newspaper, and the lady handed it over with a stern expression. Jean's mother returned to her chair and spread open the newspaper; she quickly flicked over a few pages and landed on a page with a large image of Hills Bottom Manor as its centre. Jean read the title aloud.

"Murder at the Manor."

Her mother looked at her with large eyes, magnified by her large round glasses. Her mother softly sighed and returned to her reading.

Reading this headline within another location or time may have shocked Jean, or brought back memories of Mrs Moss's contorted corpse, but the crowd of guests distracted her from internal thoughts. Jean peered through the hive of guests to meet the gaze of Robert the doorman's overwhelmed and flustered face. Robert's stunned eyes quickly flicked away from Jean to the corridor archway to the left of the staircase, the archway which that both Jean and Robert had walked through to collect a glass of warm milk from the kitchen during Jean's first night. A member of kitchen staff strode out from the kitchen corridor and into the entrance hallway, her head was fixed to the floor as with long strides she shot through the crowd of guests, she held a small bag in one hand. Robert opened the door for her, still wearing his shocked expression as he did so. This event only increased the noise of the crowd. The guests very slowly exited the manor from the now open door, each shouting their last angry goodbyes in the direction of Mrs Grey, who stood unphased behind the entrance desk.

As the last member of the crowd left, Robert slowly creaked the door closed, and the sound of two firm souled shoes hitting the stone floor brought Jean's attention to the base of the staircase.

Sergeant Lloyd stood tall with his arms out to his side with his palms up and his shoulders back. He raised his chin and eyebrows whilst looking at Mrs Grey.

"Do you have a question for us Sergeant?" Mrs Grey asked with a weary tone.

"I do, do you know where Inspector Lewis is, Mrs Grey?" Sergeant Lloyd's question was asked with a calm yet condescending or perhaps sarcastic tone, the tone was reminiscent for Jean as it reminded her of teachers at school.

"He is always by your side Sergeant Lloyd, although he may have left because of today's news, like the other guests." Mrs Grey tapped her nails on a discarded newspaper Infront of her.

Sergeant Lloyd strode forward towards the entrance desk, his overly deliberate steps clacked along the stone entrance hallway floor. With his round chest pushed out and his eye lids narrowed he peered down at the newspaper on the desk. He started to read softly, almost under his breath.

"Murder at the Manor. Mrs Iris Moss pushed to her death? It has been both a night to remember and to forget as the local residence of the quite village of Hills Bottom wake up to debate as to whether or not a murder has occurred..." Sergeant Lloyd, paused for a moment.

"This is not good for our investigation." He gave a heavy sigh and turned to face Robert. "Robert, have you seen Inspector Lewis leave the Manor this morning?"

A flustered Robert shakily replied. "No sir, I have not."

"Well then, Mrs Grey I have a favour to ask you." Announced Sergeant Lloyd. "Could you please open room 31, Inspector Lewis's Room?"

Mrs Grey disappeared below the entrance desk, for no longer than a second, before quickly re-emerging to walk at a purposeful pace in the direction of Sergeant Lloyd and the stair ways.

"It is against protocol to open a guest's room without prior warning, especially while they may be sleeping, but as you are both police officers you will have to explain this intrusion to each other." She spoke loudly over the resonating sound of her own heels clicking against the stone entrance floor.

Both Sergeant Lloyd and Robert hastily followed her up the staircase, out of Jean and her mother's sight.

By the time Robert and Sergeant Lloyd had caught up to Mrs Grey she was stood facing Inspector Lewis's room. Mrs Grey bent over, swiftly moved her key to the right and vigorously pushed the door open. Sergeant Lloyd bounded into the dark room, the curtains were drawn shut, yet thin streaks of light from the edge of the window projected themselves across the room and on to the empty bed in the corner.

Mrs Grey threw open the curtains and gestured around at the emptiness of the room. Inspector Lewis's belongings were still present in the room and placed orderly. The en-suite bathroom door was open; it was immediately obvious to the three of them that Inspector Lewis was not in Room 31.

Robert broke the silence. "Could he not have gone out for an early morning walk perhaps, there are no shoes left in this room?"

"I very much doubt it, Inspector Lewis is a well drilled police officer with impeccable time management, we were due to meet outside of my room just short of an hour ago now. I assumed that only sickness could have prevented him from keeping to our arranged time, but now I fear much worse." He paused briefly to remove is pen and notebook from his jacket pocket. "Robert could you please make your way down to the dining room and lounge areas and please let everyone know that I request for all guests to remained seated wherever they are, I shall be asking a lot of questions."

Mrs Grey interjected. "Robert, man the door. Sergeant is this really necessary, I am sure that Inspector Lewis has simply gone walking, or into the village, could his watch not have broken, there are many plausible explanations for his tardiness, there is no need to upset guests further."

Sergeant Lloyd took no notice of Mrs Grey's plea and rushed out of the room, with Robert in pursuit.

9. *Until Further Instructions*

The concentric swirly plaster patterns on ceilings can be anything, water ripples in a lake after a large stone had been thrown in, maybe mountainous plains ruled by tiny imaginary creatures, or perhaps the frowns and smiles of many faces in a crowd, The concentric swirly plaster patterns on ceilings can be anything when you are a bored eight-year-old. Jean was sat on a dining room chair, her head lent back, resting on the top of the chairs back rest, her neck at ninety degrees and her eyes staring up at the ceiling. Her Mother was a quarter of a way through reading the large pile of newspapers, which she had collected from the entrance hallway and desk.

Robert entered the dining room, his face flushed.

He loudly cleared his throat. "Unfortunately, I must ask that you all remain seated and in the dining room, until further instructions, Sergeant Lloyd, who is one of the police officers who arrived yesterday morning, would like to conduct some police work and speak to all of you. Apologies." As quickly as he had entered Robert left.

Jean's eyes lit up with the thought of excitement. Jean's Mother caught her look.

"It is no skin off our nose is it Jean, we have plenty of papers to read." She said rhetorically.

The dining room was scarcely occupied with only three tables in use, Jean and her mother sat on a square table positioned centrally yet close to the entrance, whilst the two back corners of the dining room were the breakfast places for Mr Shean and a family Jean had not seen before. Mr Shean sat modelling a pair of blue braces over a white shirt, with his bowler hat hooked on the backrest of a chair. The family at the other corner table consisted of a husband and wife with two teenage boys, once Robert had notified them of the imminent Police action, they muttered between themselves. As for Mr Shean he took little notice, it appeared not to be interesting enough to draw his attention away from his tower of breakfast pancakes.

Sergeant Lloyd had made it to the base of the staircase and was now looking down the entrance hallway, the emptiness of the hallway briefly took him aback, with all the guests being told to remain seated, he thought to himself that this would make for a few minutes of spare time. He could briefly reflect on the events of his manor visit. He looked left toward one of the thin chairs that Jean and her mother had sat on just a few moments ago. The chair creaked loudly as he lowered his weight onto it, he took his small black notebook out of his pocket, hunched over with his elbows resting on his knees, pushed the black cover to one side and began to read the first page of his notebook quietly to himself.

10. Deceased Investigation

MRS   IRIS   MOSS   -   DECEASED INVESTIGATION.

The Manor house has one main entrance and exit, fire exits shall be noted later.

Guests are greeted by two elderly members of staff upon arrival, one of which is medium build who directs cars into parking spaces, the other introduces himself as Robert, and he is of smaller build. Both men are dressed in dark green jackets that distinguish the staff from guests.

Upon entering the Manor we are also greeted by Mrs Grey, the Manager and concierge.

Mrs Grey has made clear that she does not wish for inspector Lewis and myself to spend a long time at the manor, our reception has been frosty.

We have asked for a tour of the grounds. Mrs Grey is to be our guide.

The ground floor of Hills Bottom Manor is comprised of an entrance hallway and four large rooms, a large lounge, a smaller lounge, a dining hall and a large kitchen.

Including the ground floor the manor has five floors, four floors for guest and staff bedrooms. All floors are accessed by a main staircase; the staircase has one landing area between floors three and four. The landing area is the position where Manor staff found Mrs Moss.

The Landing area is roughly twelve foot wide and eight foot deep, with twin staircases on the left and right hand sides, leading to the higher floors. The landing has one large painting placed in the centre of the main wall, the painting is of a grey-haired man sitting on a large armchair dressed in a black gown and formal hat, holding a scroll. Placed at either side of the painting there are two green armchairs.

Upon inspection of the landing there is nothing visibly odd, the only noteworthy observation is that there are faded patches where Mrs Moss was led, faded most likely from bleach from soaking the blood out of the carpet. Small patches of carpet are a lighter shade of green.

Natural wear of the carpet due to normal use is clearly visible.

After ascending to the second highest floor Mrs Grey instructs us that our rooms are to be 30 and 31. She does not indulge in pleasantries; she is quick to leave us, returning down the staircase.

Sergeant Lloyd rose from the creaking chair. He knew the first two people that required deeper questioning.

11. *To speak ill of the dead does no one well*

Jean was sat on the edge of her seat, both literally and figuratively. Her eyes were fixed to the green jacket of Robert, who stood at the entrance door; she felt that once Robert moved more interesting events would follow.

Mrs Grey had made it down the staircase and had taken a regimented position beside Robert, both staring blankly at Sergeant Lloyd as he now ambled towards them.

"Would you both join me at a table in the dining room?" Sergeant Lloyd did not wait for a response as he continued his amble.

Jean watched as Robert's brow flushed fuchsia and Mrs Grey straight expression quivered for a breath, Sergeant Lloyd's tall and round frame squeezed through the dining room doorway, followed by Robert's hunched small presence and Mrs Grey slim stiff figure. Sergeant Lloyd stood to address the room.

"Thank you for remaining seated, I do not know how long my police questioning will take, but please remain where you are unless you need the restroom, and in that case please gain the attention of either Mrs Grey or Robert who shall accompany you, hopefully this will not take long enough to extend into mealtime."

Cook was peering out from the doorway into the kitchen from the dining room.

"Cook, please take a seat and bring in the kitchen staff."

Cook scowled at Sergeant Lloyd but obeyed his request; she disappeared into the kitchen for as long as it took for the door to swing shut, before returning with two short elderly women, the three of them sat on the table closest to the kitchen doorway.

Sergeant Lloyd was far more agitated than Jean had witnessed previously, his eyes flicked around the room as he took to his seat at a dining table where Mrs Grey and Robert sat, Robert was uncomfortably fidgeting on his chair. The Sergeant withdrew his black book and pen from his uniform and began to thoughtfully scratch his thinning scalp. The manor fell silent, waiting on Sergeant Lloyd to begin his questioning, and the room shrunk as the necks of all on lookers stretched out towards the interrogation table in anticipation.

"My first question is, where did you last see Inspector Lewis?" Sergeant Lloyd's tone gave a false sense of composure, he nodded towards Robert, who sat both opposite and to the right-hand side of Sergeant Lloyd.

"I believe it was yesterday, in the evening, I could see both of you sat over at that table." Robert pointed a nervous finger at the table where Jean had witnessed the pair of policemen quiz Mrs Corsewell. "I was manning the entrance door."

With an obvious look of disappointment at Roberts answer Sergeant Lloyd raised his eyebrows in the direction of Mrs Grey.

She drew breath and tightly crossed her legs to one side under the table. "Both yourself and Inspector Lewis walked past the entrance desk at ten fifty two yesterday evening, I presumed towards your rooms as I saw you both walk up the first flight of stairs."

Without responding Sergeant Lloyd withdrew his black notebook and began to write notes in a scatty fractious fashion.

Jean made use of this pause in proceeding to give a coy look of excitement towards her mother, who peered up briefly from above her newspaper and gave a subtle brow raise of disapproval of Jean's excitement.

After the scratching of pen on paper had stopped Sergeant Lloyd continued.

"Mrs Grey, discounting yourself are there any other members of staff that have access to the room keys?"

Mrs Grey took no time for thought before promptly answering. "All members of staff are able to ask me for room keys, particularly Maisy who runs the turn down service, but three sets of keys are kept securely within the entrance hallway desk. The desk has shelves and double cabinet doors, which are locked at night-time by myself. I have made a note of the keys this morning and the only keys that are unaccountable for are the keys which are in the possession of guests".

"Miss Maisy is the only member of staff who runs the turn down service?" questioned Sergeant Lloyd.

"Yes, she is a hard worker, however today I have asked her to take the morning off and to rest in her room, as she was looking a little worn last night, most likely due to all the unrest Mrs Moss has caused."

Sergeant Lloyd gave a weak feigned smile. "To speak ill of the dead does no one well."

Both Robert and Mrs Grey shifted their eyes away from meeting the glare of Sergeant Lloyd.

After a brief awkward pause Sergeant Lloyd continued. "Well, Ms Maisy should be questioned also."

Sergeant Lloyd shot up from his chair and marched out of the dining room, after a beckoning gesture from the Sergeant both Robert and Mrs Grey rose from their seats and strode after him with panicked gaits.

Jean turned to her mother to give a mischievous grin, she slid from her chair, her shoes gave a dull thud as they hit the carpet. Her mother's eyes widened to fill her large round thin framed glasses.

Jean made it to the cold stone arched doorway that separated the hallway from the dining room, she peered down the entrance hall, just in time to catch the sight of Robert and Mrs Grey's shoes rise out of view up the staircase. Jean plodded back towards her mother's table and disapproving look.

"Well, Jean, maybe you are right, I suppose that if the policeman has left then we can too." Jean's Mother said as she pushed her chair back and collected the block of newspapers into her arms.

She met Jean on the way to the dining room entrance and guided her towards the lounge's two vacant armchairs, of which the pair were becoming more than accustomed to.

The lounge scene was dark, only alit by the fire and Mr Patel's bright shirt. The shirt was similar to his previous evening's attire, but this time featuring an even richer red pigment within parts of the pattern. As Jean twisted her neck around the armchair to glance at Mr Patel, he raised his friendly thick eyebrows to give a warm welcoming expression.

He had a pencil pressed loosely against a page of his sketch book; the thin wispy grey hairs that aged his hands matched the thin delicate pencil lines that he carved into the white of the page. Judging from the frequency of which he raised his head from his book towards Jean, she deduced that the sketch in progress was perhaps a sketch of herself or her mother.

Excitedly she slid from the armchair and cracked her hard souled shoes across the worn wood flooring of the lounge, making her way towards Mr Patel. She felt the warmth of both the fire and Mr Patel's smile.

"Hello again Miss Jean, and interesting morning is it not."

"It is certainly interesting, what are you drawing Mr Patel?" Jean's excitement brought the conversation quickly to her pressing question.

Mr Patel drew a large breath and began to slowly reply: "Well I begun to sketch two empty armchairs, but it appears that now I shall be drawing one empty armchair and another with your mother sat within it."

Without giving a response, Jean walked over to the stall placed under the square Chess table and dragged it across the room. The loud shuddering sound once again prompted Jean's Mother to let out a sharp and violent "Shhh!", and once again, Jean ignored her mother as she took her seat next to Mr Patel.

Mr Patel gave a soft deep splutter to clear his throat, his eyes then focused back on the page, feeling the expectation to draw from his audience sat beside him. He moved his pencil across to a fresh page, and begun to make strong, dark, confident curved lines.

Jean flicked her eyes between the sketchbook and her mother, the flicker of the fire's flames reflected in the lenses of her mother's large round glasses. A few diagonal strokes added shadow to her mother's blouse collar, a brush from the side of the pencil tip gave the arm chair its worn texture, and with the final faint and fine whisps of grey to show the flicker of flames within her mother's glasses, Mr Patel's pencil portrait of Ms Maple was complete.

Both Jean and Mr Patel lent back with accomplishment.

"It is a very good sketch Mr Patel."

Struck warmly by Jean's praise Mr Patel smiled wide in her direction.

"Have you drawn anything else since we last met Mr Patel?" Jean questioned.

"Oh yes I have, the rain and the wind were quite terrible throughout yesterday, but I managed to draw a few little bits and pieces while looking out through a few windows which overlook the back fields of the manor." Mr Patel gave a limp and casual hand gesture in the general direction of the fields.

He turned a few pages back in his sketch book and twisted the book diagonally to face Jean.

Jeans eyes closely examined the pages, there were many sketches scattered unsystematically across the page. Most drawings depicted sections of a grey stone wall, which enclosed a seating area outside the back of the manor, just before the fields. Mr Patel slowly begun to turn the pages. He had sketched the metal chairs and tables which sat inside the walls, one particular sketch was highly detailed, Jean could even make out the water drops hanging from an arm rest. The next page showed the drooped and wet figures of Sergeant Lloyd and Inspector Lewis, each held an umbrella but the anguish of the sideways rain upon them was captured well from Mr Patel's several sketches from different angles.

"I have overheard that one of them has lost the other, it is causing a stir." Jean softly murmured.

"They both seemed slightly lost once they arrived here, if you were to ask me." Mr Patel raised the corners of his mouth at his own jesting comment; it was a comment which passed Jean by.

"hmmm a lost man should be easy to find, he was quite big." Jean turned away from Mr Patel and looked wistfully into the fire. "Hide and seek in this Manor would be the most fun."

"It certainly would be fun, I am far too old now to play, but suppose we were to play, where would you hide?"

Jean pondered momentarily over Mr Patel's question, with her eyes closed she thought of the layouts of all the rooms she had been in since arriving at the Manor.

"I suppose the Kitchen, it was steamy in there, and there are cupboards to hide in." Jean smiled, content with her answer. "If you were my age, Mr Patel, where would you hide first?"

"Oh, if I were young, well I think I would be straight up there." Mr Patel pointed to the fireplace. "Straight up the chimney climbing the walls like a monkey."

Jean burst into laughter.

Her imaginary spectacle of Mr Patel climbing the inner walls of the fireplace were most amusing to Jean. Mr Patel softly chuckled alongside her.

Jean's Mother coughed. The laughing pair simmered down, and Jean met the gaze of her scowling Mother.

"Jean, I might go to this Kitchen you speak of to see if I can get a hold of a glass of water. Maybe you should go and sit with your mother for a little while."

"I'll come with you!" Jean blurted.

"Of course, you are welcome to, but may I suggest that you ask your mother first as to whether or not she would like you to join me." Mr Patel recommended in a reasoning tone.

Without a word Jean bounced off the stool and with a spring to her step briskly made her way to her mother's side.

"Mother, may I go with Mr Patel to the Kitchen to ask for drinks?"

Her mother kept her head down in between the sheets of the newspaper as she answered: "You may Jean."

Jean thought nothing of her mother's blunt reply, her mind was solely fixated on the joy of the small, but in her current circumstances, big adventure to the Kitchen which to Jean was an exciting moment to take her away from the boredom of sitting quietly watching her mother read newspapers.

Jean gave a nod to Mr Patel and beckoned him to her with an inward wave.

He smiled, rose from his seat and scuffled across the wooden floor. While witnessing his walk Jean realised that it would have been difficult for him to play hide and seek with her. Once Mr Patel met Jean by the lounge entrance the pair began to shuffle into the entrance hall.

It appeared that all guests and staff had very much abandoned their instructions to remain in the dining room, as Mrs Grey had returned to her post at her desk, the doorman was stood proudly at attention, and Jean could hear murmurs of conversations from every direction.

Mrs Grey paid them no attention as they walked down the entrance hall and turned right down the thin corridor where Robert had once taken her.

"I hope you don't mind, but as we are here, would you mind if I went to the bathroom?" Mr Patel asked sheepishly.

Jean had never been asked this question before, she was always the one that felt the need to ask, with a confused expression on her face, she answered softly "No, I do not mind."

"Excellent, I shall just be a moment." With these words Mr Patel turned and pushed open a blue door he was immediately adjacent to. Jean could peek through the open door at some white tiles briefly before the door drew closed.

With the mission for water still at hand, Jean felt compelled to continue onwards into the Kitchen rather than to wait for Mr Patel.

She needed all of her strength to push an opening, which was just large enough for herself to squeeze through, between the set of imposing double doors to the Kitchen. She then found herself again surrounded by the steam and noise. The heat hit her face, and her eyes took a brief second to adjust to the bright lights and white surroundings of the Kitchen.

Rather than the towering figure of Cook a new and more friendly face greeted her at the Kitchen entrance.

"Who might we have here?" Questioned a small lady, she was round with round red cheeks and a welcoming set of eyes, she was dressed head to toe in white with a white accompaniment of flour coating her hands.

Threw squinted eyes Jean replied. "My name is Jean Maple; may I ask for some water please?"

"You can ask a member of the Manor staff you know; you do not need to worry about coming all the way to the Kitchen just to see us, but of course you may have some water." The round lady scurried down a Kitchen aisle towards a giant metal sink, she selected a large glass from a shelf along the way and began to fill the glass from the sink tap, before making her way back over to Jean.

Once stood in front of Jean she extended her arm outwards offering the glass.

"Thank you very, very much, but I would also like to take back another glass for a friend."

"Say no more! I can do better than another glass!" As she finished her sentence the round lady once again pivoted and made way for the sink, but this time she selected a bulbous curved jug, as well as a second glass which matched the first. She filled the two new vessels to the top with water before cradling all three items in-between the crook of her elbow and pressed against her stomach. She then moved gingerly across the back of the kitchen to a wide metallic door, she snapped at the handle, pulling it upwards which then in turn opened the metal door, just enough so that she could stretch her unburdened arm into the room. The round lady revealed that she had collected three ice cubes from within, she dropped them into the jug. Using her hip she slammed the metal door shut and hastily made it back to stand once again in front of Jean.

The round lady handed over the three items to Jean. Jean awkwardly opened her arms and hugged all three wet glass objects to her chest; she could feel the water splashing lightly up at her chin as she edged backwards towards the door. The round lady held open one of the ominous Kitchen double doors so that Jean could make her discomfited exit.

"Bye now Mrs Maple." Said the round lady, she beamed a red blushed smile at Jean and let the door swing shut.

12. *Gruesome and devilish*

The bubbles within water glasses can be anything, planets moving around each other in a faraway galaxy, maybe bubble shaped beings that rose to the top of the glass slowly to reach the surface for air, or perhaps round bumper cars with some avoiding others which are intentionally trying to collide. The bubbles within water glasses can be anything when you are a bored eight-year-old.

Jean had been waiting outside of the blue bathroom door for an undistinguishable amount of time, she had no idea how long, as the boredom had removed her ability to judge how much time had passed. She knew that it must have been quite a while, as bubbles had appeared within the water jug, as well as the two glasses the round lady had given her. Jean was sat with her legs crossed on the corridor carpet looking at the glasses she had placed down in front of her.

Her patient perseverance to wait for Mr Patel to finish in the bathroom was at an end. She stood up slowly and stretched out her back, as she had been sat hunched over with her head in her hands for long enough to result in a tight sensation from her shoulders to her lower back. Jean twisted her shoulders and started to walk to the end of the thin corridor, so that she could peak around the corner towards the entrance door.

Mrs Grey, the Doorman and Mr Shean were all positioned in front of the entrance door. To Jean they all appeared very engrossed within their conversation. Jean walked backwards towards the blue door, now confident that if she were to sneak into the bathroom she was likely not to be seen.

The previous glimpse of white tiles and given her the desire to see more of the room behind the blue door, sitting outside it for a long time had also increased her curiosity.

Shyly she begun to slowly push open the door, she first slid her head into the white tiled room, her body shortly followed, she made sure the door shut softly behind her. The room was another short corridor leading towards an opening that was to the right, the white tiles made the room feel very bright and clean.

Jean felt compelled to call out. "Mr Patel…. Mr Patel, I have water outside."

After waiting for a response that never came, Jean felt a little embarrassed, as she now concluded that it was most likely that Mr Patel had left the room while she was collecting water. Now concerned that she could be punished for entering a bathroom without her mother, Jean briefly considered leaving the room and hesitated, but after realising that she may never see what is around the corner and through the opening she took two quick large steps forward and sharply looked right.

Red thick puddles of blood, slashes of red sprayed across the white tiles. Mr Patel's figure hung from a broken white porcelain sink, the shard remains of his teeth and jaw led open dripping over the edge. His arms and legs twisted like cracked branches, bones had broken through the skin in multiple places. His hair was matted with blood and a gash to his skull shimmered wet. His blood-shot eyes rolled into the back of his head and he let out a muffled spluttered whimper.

Jean felt empty, her hairs were on end and it was as if the blood had left her body, she staggered backwards dizzily. Jean forced her eyes closed, so that she could bring herself to turn away. She began to run. She threw open the blue door, turned the corner and sprinted at Mrs Grey, The Doorman and Mr Shean.

"HEELLLLLPP!" Jean shouted as loudly and as high pitched as she could, tears forced themselves from her eyes.

"Good lord child!" Mrs Grey shouted back.

Jean did not pause to explain, she turned and ran as fast has she could back down the entrance hall until she was once again at the blue bathroom door.

She stood head hung, pointing at the door, she could hear that Mrs Grey, Mr Shean and the Doorman had all followed her as she ran. Although Jean knew that the adults were asking her questions the pounding of her heart, the buzzing of her head and her own spluttering rendered all noise illegible.

Mrs Grey was first to push the door open, she did so in a very casual manner and stood into the white tiled room with no caution. The Doorman and Mr Shean waited in silence.

Thud!

A thud could be heard from the other side of the door.

"Mrs Grey Mrs Grey!" The two onlookers shouted before bursting the room open themselves to rush inside.

Mrs Grey had fainted.

"Oh no!"

"Christ!"

"Where is Sergeant Lloyd?!"

Mr Shean immerged from the room dragging the unconscious Mrs Grey, followed closely by the Doorman who sprinted down the corridor, with a running gait of a much younger man.

The double Kitchen doors flew open, the round lady entered only to be shouted at instantly by Mr Shean:

"Some water… some towels!"

The round lady exited, to return sharply with white towels and another jug of water.

Mr Shean rolled up a towel to place under Mrs Grey before selecting to pick up both jugs of water, both the water that had just arrived as well as Jean's previous water, and with a jug in each hand threw their contents at the face of Mrs Grey.

Mrs Grey let out a gargled shriek. "Why on earth would you do that?"

"You were unconscious Mrs Grey." Pleaded Mr Shean.

Loud stomping footsteps could be heard from the stairway. Sergeant Lloyd entered the corridor at pace. He crashed through the blue door as all other parties waited in silence.

He was gone for some time, so long that all the occupants of the Manor had gathered within the corridor. Jean's Mother gave Jean an awkward hug as the pair watched the door amongst the crowd.

A few more tense minutes passed before a forlorn Sergeant Lloyd re-emerged, to address the crowd.

"It appears we have experienced another murder."

The crowd gasped and murmured at the news.

"It is with certainty the most gruesome and devilish murder scene I have ever witnessed. Every person present will remain in the dining room until further instructions, there will be no exceptions, Manor staff shall ensure that you are all safe; all of you will be together. I shall give further instructions shortly."

The crowd begun to shuffle towards the dining room, Jean and her mother silently went with the crowd.

Sergeant Lewis stopped both Mrs Grey and the now present Robert and whispered to them: "Robert, please can you board up or block off this bathroom, no one is to enter. Mrs Grey I shall need to use the telephone."

Robert gave a confirmative nod and the still soaking, but now poised, Mrs Grey gave an affirmed look and begun to walk back to the entrance corridor.

Jean and her mother had taken up their usual two seats at a four-person dinner table. The room was quiet with no one feeling that it was appropriate to make a sound.

Due to the eerie silence every movement within the echoing entrance hall could be heard. Sergeant Lloyd was frantically winding around the number dial of the Manor's telephone, the ratchet like clicks pause briefly and then started up again.

"Mrs Grey, this telephone simply does not work."

Sergeant Lloyd's remark was closely followed by the now familiar clack of Mrs Grey's heels on the entrance hall floor. The fast ticking of the telephone dial being twisted by Mrs Grey echoed down the hallway. There was a momentary silence.

"Well, maybe a cable mast fell during yesterday's storm." Mrs Grey wishfully hypothesised.

"Mrs Grey, true, there was quite a storm yesterday, but it would be quite a coincidence for the phone lines to be down, just as a demonic murder has occurred." Sergeant Lloyd was certainly shaken; his voice had lost its monotone quality. He strode menacingly to loom over the doorman who stood at his regular post.

"Where is the nearest telephone box?"

Jean lent slightly backwards on her chair to get a better view as the Sergeant probed the Doorman.

With wide eyes and a flushed face, the Doorman shakily answered: "It's up the Hill Sir, it's a few minutes' drive or just short of half an hour's brisk walk"

The Doorman ducked underneath Sergeant Lloyd's gaze to pull open the door.

The wind once again howled into the entrance hall, with a scattering of leaves accompanying. Sergeant Lloyd stepped into the arched doorway and paused briefly. He muttered under his breath.

"Inspector Lewis has the keys." After a soft submitting sigh, he turned to face Mrs Grey, to announce his plan.

"I cannot leave the Manor when an active murderer is among us, I shall stay until I have eliminated one person from the potential suspects list, and I shall then ask this innocent person to walk to the nearest telephone box to make a call to the police station. Mrs Grey, would the Doorman and yourself please take a seat in the dining room."

Once the Doorman and Mrs Grey had silently made their way, Sergeant Lloyd lent against the entrance hall desk and withdrew his notebook.

13. Deceased Investigation - Questioning

MRS IRIS MOSS - DECEASED INVESTIGATION.

After second floor room inspections (both nothing to report) Inspector Lewis and I walk out to the third floor landing.

Each set of stairs is looked over for tripping hazards, no obvious hazards are discovered.

The carpet on the edge of all stairs are noticeably worn and faded. Floorboards are uneven beneath the carpet it is possible to feel the ridges of the floorboards. These two observations are not deemed as tripping hazards at this point in time by either myself or Inspector Lewis.

Due to statements from both the forensic personnel and the undertaker tripping appears to be more likely than the deceased being pushed. At this moment in time there are no other pieces of evidence that suggest anything other than a trip, or a push could have resulted in the death of Mrs Moss.

Inspector Lewis and I shall begin our interviews with guests at the hotel.

A small gathering of guests are within the entrance hallway, many appear to be leaving.

We position ourselves just outside the entrance door. Inspector Lewis records the details of the guests who are leaving the manor, in case we need to contact them further. Inspector Lewis records contact details. I proceed to note their appearance and their responses when questioned over Mrs Moss:

Mr and Mrs Ben Witmoore

Black pin stripe suit grey short hair, medium build, 5.7ft

Blue dress, hat and long navy coat, blonde to grey hair 5.4ft

No contact with Mrs Moss, did not leave their room during the night.

Mr and Mrs Roger Carlson

Large camel trench coat, hat, black moustache, formal trousers, green jumper. 6ft, thin build

Grey dress, brown hair, long black coat, 5·2ft.

Thought Mrs Moss looked at them oddly during dinner, thought nothing of it, did not leave their room during the night.

The Parker Family

Harry, Elizabeth and Charles

Grey haired, large, shirt with black overcoat, 5·6ft

Red hat, black hair, large, red blouse, large black overcoat 5·3ft

Charles, 9 Years old

Witnessed Mrs Moss's body on the staircase, this is their only encounter.

Three sets of guests leave during the morning, although others seem keen to exit today.

After assessing the activity within the entrance hall, Inspector Lewis and I make our way to the dining room for lunch.

The dining room is large, carpeted with eleven sets of tables and chairs, all tables are square with four chairs around them. At the back corner of the dining room there is a small bar area with a door leading to the kitchen.

We position ourselves at the bar and ask a member of kitchen staff for sandwiches. The member of staff is in a managerial role as she orders another member of staff to prepare our lunch.

Inspector Lewis asks her if she would mind answering some of our questions, interview notes are as follows:

Q: Name: 'Cook'

Mentions she does not use any name other than cook

Q: Age: 39

Q: Manor role: 'Cook' (answered resentfully)

- Cook appears very agitated by us

Q: What did you think of Mrs Moss?:

'She was not pleasant, everyone thought so everyone will back me up'

Q: Who are you referring to when you say 'Everyone'?:

'Everyone. Hotel staff, guests that spoke to her for two minutes'

Q: What exactly made you dislike her?

'Again this was not just me, she was rude, argumentative, cheap.'

Q: Cheap?:

'Yeah cheap, she stayed at the Manor for almost a month and she dressed wealthy, but always ordered bread, soup, crackers.'

Q: Being money conscious does not seem like a reason to actively dislike someone?:

'Oh there is being money conscious and then there is being cheap just to rub people up the wrong way, Mrs Moss had an odd attitude'

Q: Do you think there was a killer who could have murdered Mrs Moss:

'No I don't believe so.'

- Answered sharply

Q: You sound very sure?:

'It's unlikely, far more likely she fell,

Q: But you said people did not like her:

'We have some odd characters around but none that odd, killers wouldn't come to Hill's Bottom'

Q: Who are these 'odd characters'?:

'Well we have an Indian fellow staying and a TV salesman, also a few odd characters asked for refunds this morning just moments ago, I would question all of them if I were you.

(Cook turns to walk away)

Inspector Lewis informs her that she may go but we shall talk again to ask more questions. She does not reply.

After lunch we take a brief recess in our separate rooms and agree to meet at 15:00pm within the entrance hall.

15:00pm

We ask Mrs Grey for the name of the Indian man that Cook had previously mentioned.

Mrs Grey informs us that the man is named Mr Patel and he is seated at a writing desk in a nearby lounge area. We call him over to us to question him, Inspector Lewis leads the conversation. Interview notes are as follows:

Q: Name: Mr Patel, however this is not his real name but his 'known' name

[he speaks with a heavy Indian accent]

Q: Real Name, spelt: B H A R A T   D A R R U W A L A

Q: Why use an alias?: 'British people are warm to the name Patel, Daruwala is confusing over here'

[Odd statement]

Q: Would It not be true in stating that simply the letter D would be even less confusing, or for example a shortening such as DAR. Then we British would have less letters to find potentially confusing?:

- 'I did not mean that British people in particular would find Daruwala confusing, but British people have most often heard of the name Patel before and the familiarity is reassuring.'

Q: I know that if I moved to India I would still refer to myself as Mr Lewis. When did you arrive at Hill's Bottom Manor?: 'I arrived three weeks ago.'

Q: Where were you before this? 'Monmouth, at a B and B'

Q: Where are you heading Mr Darruwala?: 'Nowhere in particular I have travelled all my life and wish to continue to do so.'

Q: Do you understand that this can be considered suspicious behaviour, I could hypothesise that you are moving around to avoid something?: 'Only moving around to avoid the boredom of old age.'

[Said jokily, deflecting the serious nature of our questioning]

Q: I think we should remind you that this is a potential murder investigation; did you have any encounters with Mrs Moss during your three weeks here? 'She dared not look at me, we never spoke.'

Interruption - A tall Lady with a teal dress has made a disturbance behind us. She places keys on the entrance hallway desk, she is leaving in a hurry.

Mr Darruwala: 'That seems like suspicious behaviour'

I interject to assure Mr Darruwala that he is our focus at this moment in time.

Inspector Lewis points out the Mr Darruwala is looking very suspicious:

- He sticks out within the manor
- He moves around frequently
- He claims to have not spoken to the deceased, ever
- He has invented a fake name

Q: Is there any other information you feel you should tell us Mr Darruwala?:

'I am far too old to bring any trouble upon myself or to cause any trouble upon anyone else.'

Q: How old are you Mr Darruwala?:

'I am 71 years old'

Q: Can we ask where you were at the time Mrs Moss was alleged to fall?:

'I was asleep, I awoke to the sound of screaming, once I had moved over to the door to take a look outside my room, I could see that guests were heading back into their rooms'

Q: Did you not go outside your room?:

'No I did not'

Q: Did any guest see you looking out of your doorway?:

'I suppose they might have seen my door open slightly'

Q: So it is likely that no other guest or staff member can back up your claim that you were in your room?:

'I am not sure this questioning is fair officers'

I interject to assure Mr Darruwala that as a police officer fairness is one of the highest priorities.

Inspector Lewis calls a halt to the questioning.

We decide to ask Mrs Grey as to whether she has contact information for a Mrs Corsewell, who we are aware owns the Manor.

Mrs Grey mentions that Mrs Corsewell lives at the Manor, and eats dinner every day on a far table within the dining room.

We also ask Mrs Grey for the contact information for the Lady dressed in teal who left angrily, before repositioning ourselves at a table near the bar of the dining room.

Inspector Lewis and I agree that a murder is looking more and more likely.

After a long wait, during which we also ate, Mrs Corsewell arrives. We give her a moment to finish a meal that has been brought to her, then we begin our questioning. Inspector Lewis leads the interview: I take notes, which are as follows:

Q: Good evening, Mrs Corsewell:

'I have heard that your presence is upsetting the guests, do not upset guests"

Q: Unfortunately protocols must be taken Mrs Corsewell:

'Well what is best for the manor opposes the views of policemen, an old lady fell, old ladies fall, I am far more aware of that than you both, I'm sure you will agree'

[very defensive]

Q: How old do you think Mrs Moss was?:

'Old enough to fall'

Q: Did you ever meet Mrs Moss?:

'I rarely meet with guests; I keep myself to myself and focus on other matters'

Q: Has an accident like this happened before?: 'On occasions guests have tripped and fallen, but nothing to report'

I point out that she is answering angrily

'Yes I am angry, I am angry that you have forced yourselves upon us and I am angry at Mrs Moss, for her carelessness is the root of this.'

Inspector Lewis continues stating that police must ask questions and assess the scene

Mrs Corsewell: 'You should do so during normal working hours'

Inspector Lewis mentions the following:

-A lot of guests saw Mrs Moss on the staircase.

-Everyone may have to be questioned

- We have been met with an odd attitude by everyone we have spoken to.

- It is strange that individuals mention disliking Mrs Moss

'From what I hear Mrs Moss was not a pleasant woman and brought it on herself.' Direct quote.

I Question Q: Brought what on herself madam?" 'Brought the distaste of others upon herself, she tell officers, now may I retire to my room for the rest of the day?"

Inspector Lewis calls a halt to the interview.

Sergeant Lloyd moved from the desk and placed the black notebook back into its regular position within his lapel pocket. He paced into the dining room.

14. Who's next?

Jean was no longer bored, her mind battled thoughts. She thought over all the events that led to her entering the bathroom with a blue door, she thought of Mr Patel's sketch book, she thought of Mr Patel's warm and friendly presence, she thought of Mr Patel's lifelessly hanging jaw.

In her thoughtful haze she looked up, the caught the sight of her mother's eyes, despite her holding a fiction book up almost pressed to her face Jean's mother peered over the pages with her round lenses. She was looking past Jean, her attention fixed on events behind their table.

Jean turned.

Sergeant Lloyd was surrounded, surrounded both physically by the other occupants of the dining room and surrounded by their sound as they shouted towards him. He had his back pressed tightly against a wall and wore his most reassuring expression.

After a moment spent regaining herself from her thoughts Jean started to pick up on words that had made their way through the rattled hum of noise:

"And now we are all in this mess!"

"How have you lost your friend?"

"Who's next?"

"Call the station!"

Mrs Grey, with Cook stood alongside her silenced the noise with a question addressed to all.

"Who would like lunch?" With a much softer tone she continued: "As we all may be here a while"

In an awkward fashion the guests and Manor staff made their way to tables, muttering within their groups. Cook marched around the tables, collecting orders.

Jean recognised all inhabitancies of the dining room; Mr Shean sat alone at a table, the main doorman and Robert sat together, Miss Maisy and the round kitchen lady lent on the bar situated at one side of the dining room. The family Jean had previously seen with teenage boys remained within their back corner, both Mrs Grey and Sergeant Lloyd took a seat at separate tables.

Sergeant Lloyd had taken a seat at the table closest to the entrance but had turned his chair to face the room. He leant over to one side to write notes within his book.

Cook had made her way to Jean and her mother's table.

"Lunch?" She said blankly.

"We shall have two tomato soups please." Replied Jean's Mother.

Cook simply gave a nod and moved on.

"Cook!" Sergeant Lloyd shouted

"When preparing lunch please my I ask that only one member of manor staff leaves this room, only one personnel within the kitchen at a time."

Cook shrugged slightly and strode towards the bar, disappearing into the kitchen through a door at the back of the bar area.

"Doorman, please may I have a word?" Sergeant Lloyd gestured to the Doorman beside Robert, who quickly shot up from his seat, gave Sergeant Lloyd a sharp, short and overconscientious bow before moving to take a seat at the Policeman's table.

"May I ask for your name?"

A brief pause occurred as The Doorman collected himself, before he begun to sheepishly talk with Sergeant Lloyd.

"My name is David Wardell."

"And for how long have you worked at Hills Bottom Manor?" As Sergeant Lloyd got into the rhythm of his questioning Jean's thoughts moved away from the events of the room, she thought back to Mr Patel's sketch book.

She could not remember as to whether or not Mr Patel had picked up the sketch book from the drawing table. To Jean it felt a little odd that his book was most likely left open never to be completed or seen by its owner again. It also seemed odd to her that a lifeless Mr Patel remained not too far away from the dining room where she calmly sat. She peered down at the white of the tablecloth and thought back to the red and white tiles of the blue door bathroom.

The Doorman's, Mr Wardell's, voice was sounding more upbeat, Jean lifted her head up and began to, once again, listen to the police interview taking place.

"…..and then you see after I made such a frightful mess of that trifle Mrs Corsewell thought it best I remained at the entrance door." Mr Wardell laughed to himself as Sergeant Lloyd smiled back at him, before his expression quickly changed. The Sergeant rose from his seat.

"Mrs Corsewell! We are missing Mrs Corsewell! Miss Maisy." Miss Maisy stood tall with attention and gave Sergeant Lloyd a wide-eyed stare.

"Miss Maisy can I please ask for you to fetch Mrs Corsewell, as quickly as you can?" Miss Maisy did not slow down proceedings with a response; she rushed from the dining room. Mrs Grey sighed.

Sergeant Lloyd continued: "Mr Wardell please may I ask for you to return back to your position by the entrance door, please let know one exit the manor without my permission. Also, in the unlikely event that these guests' misfortunes are a result of your actions then we can all feel safe, as most of us can see the entrance hall door from our seats within the dining room. No funny business."

"Manning the door right away sir." Once he had repeated his orders Mr Wardell took to his position.

Jean watched as he stood up tall with his back against the large door, he now exuded a guard dog demeanour, rather than a Doorman's.

It did not take long before the angry strides of Mrs Corsewell were heard entering the dining room. Mrs Corsewell sported a similar outfit to before, although this time she appeared to have made an extra effort, with the inclusion of more rings and long dangling earrings. Her face was as scowled as ever.

"I hear that another guest has had an accident at the hotel." She spat the words.

"I do not here the empathy in your voice Mrs Corsewell, sit down and I shall inform you of the sickening details." Sergeant Lloyd was clearly no longer carefully considering his words; his voice was raised, and his hand shook as he gestured for Mrs Corsewell to sit opposite him.

Sergeant Lloyd addressed the room.

"I shall be sending Miss Maisy out to the telephone box, if in the unlikely event that these Murders…"

"Guests! An old woman fell! It was not a murder" Interrupted Mrs Corsewell, shouting with her crackling voice.

Instead of being baited into a shouting competition Sergeant Lloyd composed himself to make a second attempt at his statement addressed to the room.

"A woman is dead, a man has been gruesomely beaten to death, in the most horrific manor, and a police officer is missing. I would strongly suggest that all members of this room do not play down these events, as failure to take these proceeding seriously could result in further loss of life."

Mrs Corsewell appeared to cross her arms and legs with acceptance of the severity of the situation. Sergeant Lloyd continued.

I shall be sending Miss Maisy out to the telephone box, as she is a young girl and as she is a member of staff her whereabouts can always be confirmed by another individual, I believe her to be the least capable of these murders at this moment in time." Sergeant Lloyd reciprocated Miss Maisy's wide-eyed stare coupled with a beckoning backwards nod, she rushed towards him.

As Miss Maisy approached him Sergeant Lloyd extended out his hands and placed them on to her shoulders, he towered over her and lowered his voice.

"I am told that there is a telephone box in the village, which is half an hour's walk from The Manor, do you know of this telephone box?" Miss Maisy gave a confident nod; her face was as pale and blank as ever.

"Excellent, well, please may I ask you to call this number." Sergeant Lloyd withdrew a card from his trouser pocket. "This is the number for the South Wales police station, please explain the whole situation in as much detail as you can to the phone operator, please alert them to the fact that there is another deceased member of the public and a police officer, who is named Inspector Lewis, missing. Please pass on any messages for me once you return."

Without confirmation Miss Maisy briskly disappeared out of the dining room and into the hallway, she quickly re-emerged having put on a large grey overcoat and an emerald scarf.

"Mr Wardell, please allow Miss Maisy to exit the Manor, she is to telephone South Wales police station." Sergeant Lloyd instructed.

Without delay Mr Wardell took one long stride to his side, whilst pulling the door open. The wind barged in and rattled the halls of the Manor. Miss Maisy shuffled outside apprehensively. Mr Wardell firmly closed the door behind her.

With Miss Maisy on her mission Sergeant Lloyd turned and began to softly talk with Mrs Corsewell. With Jean straining to decipher their hushed conversation she once again found herself thinking of Mr Patel.

She wondered if there were many more sketch books, she wondered if they were within his hotel room and she wondered what places, people and objects filled their pages. If such books existed, she thought it was a shame that others would not be able to see them as she had been able to. She wondered if he had many more shirts with geometric patterns, and she wondered if all Indians were like Mr Patel. Jean also wondered as to whether Mr Patel had any enemies or perhaps whether Mr Patel was the enemy for another individual. She wondered whether or not Mr Patel was a spy or the victim of espionage. Jean was sad that she may not be able to discover the answers to her wondered questions. She had enjoyed her time with Mr Patel very much, he was certainly the most interesting character she had met for a long time.

Jean's thoughts were disturbed by a shrill screech of a sentence coming from Mrs Grey, who had slightly risen from her seat.

"I am sorry Sergeant Lloyd! But I do not believe it is fair to question Mrs Corsewell in this way, I can vouch for her character as she is a delight to work for and I have never known her to wish harm on others."

Sergeant Lloyd drew a breath to calm himself before responding. "Mrs Grey, my questioning is not a pleasant experience as we are within a very unpleasant situation, at this moment in time I am not accusing any one specific person of murder, but everyone is a person of interest."

Robert stood from his seat, shuddering the chair back across the carpet as he rose.

"Sergeant Lloyd may I speak?"

Sergeant Lloyd shrugged his shoulder and gave a feigned smile as a sign for Robert to continue.

"I too wanted to assure you of Mrs Corsewell's good character, I too have never experienced Mrs Corsewell to be violent or wish harm on others."

Sergeant Lloyd now standing tall had not withheld his pokerface.

"Robert, Mrs Grey, it is noted that you both believe Mrs Corsewell to be a morally just person, but it is also noted that you both say this from the biased position of being within her employment."

Mrs Corsewell joined in with her take on proceedings.

"Sergeant Lloyd, it appears I have two individuals who are willing to speak favourably in regards to my character. I also knew nothing of the unfortunate murder of Mr Patel until Miss Maisy informed me, as I have been in my room from late morning, so it appears I am looking most innocent, especially as I presume that there were many people positioned on the ground floor at the time of the murder."

The strain of frustration was apparent from the expression Sergeant Lloyd wore.

"Can you provide a witness, to confirm that you were within your room at the time of the murder?"

"Yes after breakfast I left through the Kitchen and said my goodbyes to both Cook and Mrs Wells"

"If Cook and Mrs Wells, were to confirm this that still would not give you a proven alibi as they did not see you go into your room."

Cook heard her name mentioned, she decided to become involve within the mass conversation.

"I can confirm her statement, I can hear the stairs creak from the kitchen, she walked upstairs. You will have to make up another story Sergeant."

Shocked and now far from composed Sergeant Lloyd gave a red-faced response.

"Police Officers do not make up stories, just ask questions to gather facts, we do not assume, I am doing my Job."

"I'm not sure that you are!" Shouted Mr Shean from his position at the back of the dining room.

"I beg your pardon!" Sergeant Lloyd shouted back.

To further explain himself Mr Shean continued, standing and slowly walking forwards as he did so:

"Well, a murder as occurred, while a police officer was within the manor, this does not appear to prove that you are protecting the public, it seems quite the contrary."

Sergeant Lloyd opened his mouth, but Mr Shean quickly resumed his explanation.

"Also, from what I hear, the death of Mrs Moss could have been an accidental fall, so it is likely that no murders happened, until you arrived that is. To further my suspicions, you have lost your partner, how does a grown man disappear. It is just my opinion, but I feel that it is you, Sergeant that should be explaining yourself. What a show it would be for a policeman to be a murderer."

Jeans Mother gave Jean a look with widening eyes, like Jean she too was captivated by the heated discussions being shouted across the room.

The now scarlet Sergeant Lloyd replied loudly through gritted teeth.

"You are all looking deeply suspicious to me, I hope for your sake Mr Shean that your comments were in jest. I do not know where Inspector Lewis is, but I feel it is now obvious that his disappearance is the result of the actions of the murderer hiding amongst us. Cook is a suspicious character with plenty of murder weapons at her disposal, Mrs Grey has keys to every room, Robert is constantly walking the halls, Mrs Corsewell has an active dislike for her guests and does not appear empathetic when discussing the murders that have occurred within her property, the guests within this manor are odd to say the least and the lower members of staff are easily capable of gaining access to rooms or murder weapons and also have an odd temperament about them. Everyone is a suspect!"

As his rant drew to an end a cauldron of noise swelled, everyone within the dining room shouted there fearful and aggrieved comments across the room.

Jean winced at the eruption; she could not make out the entirety of what was said but caught snippets that carried threw the discourse.

"Maybe Inspector Lewis is hiding, waiting to kill us one by one!"

"It is obviously not my intention to murder those who do not buy a TV!"

"A family could easily be killers; they're more of them to work together!"

"As a policeman I took an oath!"

"Mrs Grey is indeed a stern and cold woman!"

"Kitchen knives would cut a man to ribbons!"

"Anyone of any size can push an old lady!"

"Robert is the only person who has been outside today!"

The harshly yelled phrases continued, pained by the noise Jean moved her hands over her ears. She tightly sealed her fingers and thumbs to prevent the noise from breaking through.

15. *Stared down at the red liquid*

An echoing clang reverberated through the entrance hall and silenced the dining room.

Miss Maisy had returned.

Mr Wardell closed the door, with a similar resonant clang.

Miss Maisy edged into the room, her coat soaked through, corpulent drops fell to the carpet. Sergeant Lloyd walked over. Jean had now removed her hands from her ears, she listened intently to the conversation taking place near her table.

"Did you make it through to South Wales?" Eagerly questioned a slightly relieved Sergeant Lloyd.

Miss Maisy spoke with a hushed, soft and fluttery voice. "I did, they will be sending two more police officers over tomorrow morning, as well as a crime scene team."

"Tomorrow, not right away?" Sergeant Lloyd looked puzzled.

"Yes, they said they would deal with it properly in the morning, they mentioned that you should make sure no one leaves the Manor and that everyone else is safe." With her message complete Miss Maisy begun to unravel her scarf.

"Uh, I see, thank you very much for making the call." Whilst looking a little defeated Sergeant Lloyd slowly returned to his seat.

The other members of the dining room had relaxed; they had also taken to their seats. The round lady, now named as Mrs Wells, who Jean had received the water from, had begun to deliver plates of food to each table. Although, once Miss Maisy had dropped her dripping coat and scarf across the bar top, she took over the delivery duties from Mrs Wells. Jean hypnotically watched the repetition of Mrs Wells emerging from the kitchen to place a plate on the bar top; Miss Maisy would collect the plate, walk through the dining room and place it carefully down in front of the recipient, who would give a softly spoken thank you in return.

Miss Maisy continued to do this until she collected her last two white plates; two small bowls were concentrically positioned on top of the plates, each plate had a round dusty brown bread roll perched on the edge. Miss Maisy placed the bowls in front of Jean and her mother. Jean's mother gave the customary thank you as Jean stared down at the red liquid. Tomato soup.

Jean thought back to the red tiles.

A splatter of soup had made its way from the bowl onto the plate beneath; Jean licked her finger after wiping away the speckling of red soup. She wondered if the blood would be wiped just as easily from the tiles, would they once again be as white as the plate.

Jean felt a tight squeeze on her arm, her mother was glaring towards her, the red of the soup reflected like a red crescent moon sunk in the bottom half of her round framed glasses.

"Jeeeean." She drew out Jean's name as she spoke to give a stern impression.

Jean looked underneath her mother's looming figure, her mother had finished her bowl of soup, with the only evidence of a bread roll being a few scattered crumbs on a plate. Jean realised that this was her mother's way of telling her to eat her soup faster. Lost in her daydream within the soup she had not realised the speed of time passing. Jean hastily finished her tepid meal.

After the hurried lunch, Jean assessed the room for changes. Guests and staff a like appeared subdued and jaded, the two teenage boys belonging to the family that occupied the far corner table had their foreheads pressed to the placemats. To Jean people appeared bored, and a little frustrated. Sergeant Lloyd was speaking softly to Mrs Crosewell, who had kept her scowl firmly fixed towards the Sergeant. Jean strained but she could not make out the conversation, the rest of the room was silent. Certain in the fact that she would not be able to endure sitting patiently for what could be hours, Jean felt the need to speak.

"Mother." Jean's Mothers nose and eyes rose from behind a newspaper. "Could we, well, would we be allowed to sit on the green armchairs?"

As she spoke, Jean did not lower her voice. The room turned to face Jean, and then all shifted their attention to Sergeant Lloyd. Jean's mother looked over her shoulder to join in on the expected stare the room gave Sergeant Lloyd.

"These interviews may take some time, so you can all now stretch your legs, anyone can move into other public areas of the Manor, however no one is to go back into their guest rooms, and on the condition that no singular person is left on their own. This means there must be always at least two people within rooms, including bathrooms. I shall be counting on Manor staff to both help with this request and enforce it. If anyone witnesses anything suspicious, please alert me immediately."

Without hesitation Jean slid from her chair and pounded strides across the dining room carpet. She clacked the heels of her small black derby shoes against the smooth stone of the hallway and found herself at the entrance of the lounge. She stood still for a moment peering into the empty room. Mr Patel's sketchbook sat unmoved on the writing desk, unaffected by the proceedings of the last few hours. Jean's mother had followed, and now stood beside Jean.

Jean looked up at her mother.

"Mr Patel's sketchbook."

Jean's mother assumed the question behind this vague statement.

"Well Jean, I think you can keep it, maybe he would have let you have it anyway, we shall never know."

Delighted with her mother's slight encouragement Jean made her way to the writing desk. The fire within the room had burnt out, the room was no longer warmly lit by the flames, and the room was far colder than it had been during her previous visits. Jean looked down at the closed sketchbook and paused briefly before sliding it from the table and under her arm. She turned to look at the square table which displayed the chess board upon it; another piece was positioned sideways. To Jean it was one of the more interesting pieces as it resembled a tall thin castle, it led slightly over hanging the board.

"Come on Jean!" Her mother summoned her to the lounge entrance, where she still stood. As Jean walked over to her, she wore a puzzled expression as her mother had not yet occupied one of the green leather armchairs.

"Why don't we go outside for a little while, before it turns to dusk?" Her mother asked rhetorically.

Puzzled still Jean questioned: "Are we allowed?"

"Well, I suppose so, as I have just seen one of the elderly male members of staff walk toward the back door." With hast her mother turned back into the entrance hall. Jean caught up and walked beside her down the hallway, they took a left past the main staircase, the pair were abruptly stopped by a glass paned door. Jean pressed her nose to the glass as a handful of rain drops hit against it.

"Put this on Jean, I believe they are for guests." Her Mother said as she flung Jean a large mottled green hunting coat. Jeans Mother took a longer, but otherwise identical coat from a black iron hanger beside the glass door, she proceeded to wrap the coat around her. Jean awkwardly mimicked her mother, but with less grace due to the complexity of also carrying Mr Patel's sketch book. Jean looked down at the bottom edges of the coat folded on the stone floor, and she looked at her one free hand, which was completely engulfed by the mud green sleeve.

"It may be on the large side Jean, but I can assure you it will keep you warm out there." As she finished her consoling statement Jean's mother twisted the handle of the glass paned door, the wind howled in. Jean could feel her cheeks tweak as the draft caught them, she followed her mother outside.

The pair were now within a stone walled courtyard, with a few metal chairs and tables pushed to one side. There was a gap within the stone wall which made way for a view out across the fields. Jean felt a dusting of rain beginning to fall on her hair, ears and on the back of her neck, she looked down at Mr Patel's sketchbook. Half a dozen water drops had settled on the cover of the book, Jean opened her jacket to form a protective shelter and began to trudge across the courtyard towards the chairs. Her hair blew wildly across her face.

As Jean sat she felt the discomfort of the cold and wet metal seat. Jean held one arm rigidly out in front of her, gripping onto the edge of the hunting coat to continue to shelter the sketchbook from the elements. She placed the book on her knee and began to cumbersomely turn the pages with her one free hand. Before long she had made her way to the sketches of metal chairs, tables and stone walls, she looked around at her setting, feeling gratified of her accidental discovery of the courtyard area Mr Patel had sketched previously. She thought that it would be a wonderfully exciting adventure to rediscover all the places Mr Patel had sketched within his sketchbook. Her day dreaming was interrupted by shouting from her mother.

"What are you doing up there?"

Jean turned and looked around, panicked that her mother may be directing her shouting towards her.

Jean's mother was stood at the bottom of a ladder, with Robert placed at the top.

"It is rather windy to be at the top of a ladder don't you think, and should you not be keeping an eye on guests?" Jean's Mother shouted over the howl of the wind.

Robert replied gingerly. "Well, you see I am attempting to strike this blasted sack with this stick."

Robert stopped his explanation to swing at tree branch at a large hessian sack which had snagged itself on an iron bolt, the bolt protruded from the brickwork of the Manor, presumingly positioned originally for a purpose which it was no longer needed for.

"It gave poor Mrs Corsewell an awful scare in the early hours of this morning." The sack blew in the wind, hitting against the nearest window, creating a frantic tapping noise.

It reminded Jean of Mrs Moss's pen.

"Very well!" Jeans Mother shouted up at Robert as she turned to walk across the courtyard, she continued walking past Jean through the gap in the stone wall.

Jean considered whether her mother expected her to follow, but as she had hesitated for too long while making her conclusion, she thought it best to remained seated on the metal chair.

Jean continued to flick through the pages of Mr Patel's Sketchbook, whilst occasionally looking up from the sheets to update herself on the progress Robert was making. Robert would stretch out his right arm and swing back and forth rhythmically until he was certain that he could not reach the sack, at this moment he would pause for breath, Jean would then turn her attention back to Mr Patel's book. After a moment of artistic appreciation, Jean raised her head again to witness Robert having ventured up another step on the ladder, once again swinging rhythmically at the sack swaying just out of reach. Jean continued this pattern for a few cycles, until she heard the deep thud of the tree branch striking the sack. The sack caught the wind and glided across the fields, sinking to the grass for brief periods of rest before being lifted into the air and spiralling onwards. Robert eased himself slowly towards the ground, his fine wisps of grey hair flipped back and forth. Once positioned safely on the ground Robert gripped onto the steps of the ladder tightly, lifting it from its roots, he carefully carried the ladder away, around a corner of the manor and out of Jean's sight.

Without the distraction of Robert, and without the nuisance of spitting rain, which had now stopped, Jean opened the sketchbook to the next double spread of drawings. Mr Patel had filled this particular set of pages with sketches of trees, trees of all different types. Jean enjoyed the detailed drawings of bark the most, as the bark created the most intricate grey paths and patterns. She turnover the page to reveal flowers, she examined each one carefully and imagined what colours they might be. Jean felt that the flowers within these pages must be from locations near the manor, but she was unsure as to how certain her theory was. Jean decided that she would peer over the edge of the courtyard's stone wall, just in case the flowers depicted within Mr Patel's sketches were nearby. She slid from the metal chair, flicking droplets onto the courtyard's stone floor as she did so. Once at the wall she assessed the height of it, she was able to rest her chin comfortably on top, she quickly drew back as the texture of damp moss under her chin was a little unpleasant. Jean placed her hands on top of the wall and jumped into pushing herself on top of it, with her stomach pressing tenderly into the stonework, she peered over the wall. No flowers, only fields.

"Get down." Her Mother's voice cut through the wind.

Jean scraped down the wall and raced towards the metal chair to collect the sketchbook placed on top of it. Jean's Mother was striding in the direction of the glass door that led back into the Manor; she was not slowing pace to account for Jean running behind her.

Once back inside the warmth of the Manor Jean's mother took the green overcoat from Jean and, along with her own, placed them both back onto their iron hooks. The glass door rattled open as Robert also re-entered the manor.

He gave them both a gentle smile. "The light has just begun to fade out there, time to settle in for the night."

"Indeed." Replied Jean's mother.

Robert weaved between them both and made for the entrance hallway, his walk was slow but with intent.

Jean and her mother made their way back to the lounge area, and once again sat within the leather armchairs. The fire was lit, with the orange light flicking across Jean's Mother's round glasses as she continued to read yet another new paper.

Jean attempted to position the sketchbook in a comfortable manner across her knees, without the armrest of the chair interfering, it was an impossible task. As she wriggled to find a comfortable arrangement the pages of the book flopped to the side, to prevent the book from becoming further unbalanced Jean placed both hands quickly down onto the open pages of Mr Patel's sketch book. The sketch of Mr Shean stared out at her, this time around she was able to assess the sketch in greater detail, she looked closely at the image. With her nose to the page, she felt it odd how these particularly unassuming grey lines depicted Mr Shean so accurately once the viewer looked from a further distance, but with her eyes almost touching the paper all she saw were different thicknesses of grey pencil lines.

Jean's head shot up from the book at the sound of shoes pounding the stone floor of the entrance hall, rapid cracking echoed. The two teenage boys, which were part of the corner table family, were racing up and down the entrance hall. Miss Maisy watched on from her post leaning on the arch way, which separated the hallway and lounge area. Miss Maisy paid the boys no attention and continued to stare blankly into space.

Jean looked over towards the window seats, she could see the crows circling in the grey sky in front of the Manor. a tuft of brown curls appeared to be growing from the top of one of the window seats. Jean felt that it must be Mr Shean and before she considered her next cause of action her curiosity had overwhelmed her as she had begun walking over to the window seats.

"Hello again Jean." Mr Shean said somewhat reluctantly with Jean stood before him.

"Hello again Mr Shean, I was just looking at the sketch of you that I showed to you the other evening."

"Yes, I remember." Jean felt the lack of excitement within his voice.

"Would you not like to look at it again?" She questioned.

"No thank you I am fine, I have a mirror within my room, and I can now see my reflection within the windows, I am aware of what I look like."

Puzzled Jean continued with her questioning. "Do you not like it?"

Mr Shean sighed as he answered. "It is a great sketch, but I prefer my pictures to do other things."

"What other things?"

Slightly more uplifted in spirit by being asked about his thoughts Mr Shean sat up slightly and met Jean's gaze. "I want my pictures to sing, or dance, or sing and dance combined, fall in love, fight evil…"

Jean interrupted with another question. "Do you like plays and the theatre?"

Mr Shean smiled wide. "Television is much like the theatre, although you always have the best seat in the house."

Jean thought back to her wish for the manor to own a television that she could watch whenever she liked. "I do like television; I do like stories."

Mr Shean was eager to agree. "Television is like a story book, but you have the additional fun of seeing everything that happens. You can show so much more on television than you could ever read in a story book, and there are even a few shows where someone will read the stories to you."

Jean's eyes had lit up. "Do you know of any stories Mr Shean?"

Slightly taken a back Mr Shean confidently nodded.

"You must be great at telling stories as you know so much about television."

Mr Shean enjoyed the praise. "I do sometimes believe I have what it takes to be on the other side of the black and white screen."

"Do you have any stories you could tell me now? Asked Jean.

Still beaming with the thought of himself on television Mr Shean obliged. "Yes sure, why not, I believe I have the perfect story for this occasion, perhaps a story the police officers should hear also."

Jean sat down on the floor with folded legs, and awaited Mr Shean's opening line.

16. Gelert the hound

"Once upon a time there was a Prince, and this particular Prince was very fond of hunting, and he was good at it too, the best hunter in all of Wales.

This Prince had many hunting dogs which joined him during his hunting expeditions, he treasured every one of his dogs, but one in particular was his favourite, this hounds name was Gelert. Gelert had been given to the Prince by the King, as the King was so impressed with his hunting skills.

The Prince is happily married to his Princess, she has just been blessed with a new born baby son, they could not be happier.

One day the Prince begins to set off on one of his usual hunting adventures, but this time the Princess mentions that she would enjoy going with him on the adventure, although she does not think it would be wise for her to join in as there would be no one to watch the baby. The Prince would like the Princess to join the hunt and explains that he could leave his favourite hound Gelert next to the cot to guard over their baby; he trusts Gelert deeply and ensures his Princess that no harm will come to their young son. Content with this suggestion the Princess prepares herself for the hunt as the Prince sets Gelert to guard the sleeping child.

The hunting trip is a huge success and both the Prince and Princess return during the evening in joyous spirits, but when they reach the door of their home they realise that all is not well."

Jean rocked forwards onto her knees, captivated.

"As they creaked open the door they saw, blood!"

Jean went white, as she thought back to the sight of Mr Patel's blood dripping from the ends of the broken bones, that jarred out from his punctured skin.

"The blood trail led them to the cot where Gelert stood, blood dripping from his muzzle. Their baby was missing.

The Prince drew his sword and with deep despair and a tear in his eye he killed his favourite hound. As Gelert fell he let out a final yelp, in response a baby's cry could be heard from the dark corner of the room. The Prince and Princess moved toward the shadowed corner where they found their unharmed son, lying by the side of a giant wolf which lay motionless on the ground, with bite marks and blood across its entire body. The Prince realised that Gelert had killed the wolf to defend the baby, but had died by his master's sword.

The Prince was forever full of grief and remorse and never smiled ever again. The End."

Mr Shean lent backwards into his chair with a proud grin at the completion of his story.

Jean was silent.

17. Welling in her eyes

Jean sat silent and still on the wooden lounge floor.

Mr Shean leaned over to her. "It is a great story is it not, it is short, but I do like the twist at the end."

Although she was deep in contemplation, Jean did enjoy being told stories, even though she was puzzled by this one.

"It is a good story, but it is not a happy ending." Jean stated in her slight confusion.

"Well, it depends on how you look at it, for a moment we all thought the new baby was killed, but in the end it turn out to be safe and well."

Jean thought for a second and then felt compelled to agree with Mr Shean's explanation.

 "Yes, that is a nice surprise at the end." Jean felt the colour returning to her cheeks.

A growling sound murmured. It came from behind Mr Shean. Mr Shean gave Jean a baffled look, he sat still. Jean felt uneasy.

A sharp bark followed. Mr Shean leapt from his chair, with Jean shooting to her feet.

"A wolf!" Jean cried.

Giggling followed, the two teenage boys immerged from behind the window seats, both sniggered and laughed as they ran out of the lounge.

With a sense of embarrassment welling in her eyes Jean plodded over to her mother, whilst Mr Shean tentatively took to his seat.

Jean placed her chin on top of her mother's chair's arm rest.

"What was that all about Jean?" Her Mother stared directly into Jean's eyes.

"Mr Shean was telling a scary story and then the two boys made us both jump." Jean explained with a quiver.

"I see. Well maybe it would be wise for you to sit quietly for a moment and calm down; we shall go to dinner in an hour or so."

Jean obliged to her mother's suggestion and climbed upon the opposite armchair, she creaked the leather as she wriggled into a comfortable position, and then sat in silence, although her mind was busy, full of thoughts. She thought back to the sight of the lifeless Mr Patel, it seemed strange that it this moment in time he was likely to be just as she left him. She wondered whether he could have possibly been killed by a wolf, she asked herself questions:

"Do wolves live in Wales? Do Wolves live in fields or within woods? Could a wolf venture into Hills Bottom manor without being noticed? How big are wolves?" Whilst she pondered the feasibility of a wolf attack the other members of the Manor remained mostly stationary, with the occasional clacking of footsteps sounding across the entrance hall, breaking the dull silence, as the inhabitancies of the Manor infrequently used the rest room, as each pair of footsteps were followed a few minutes later by another set sounding in the reverse direction. The hour passed quickly for Jean.

Whilst still deep in thought her mother led Jean into the dining room, where they once again sat on their familiar table. Jean could look to her left to see Mr Wardell occasionally pass across the doorway to the dining room, as he paced back and forth along the entrance hall, Jean could also look out across the dining room.

The room appeared to have changed very little during the hours Jean had been away, although the room felt tired. Guests sat either hunched over or were sat back within their seats and only managed to softly mumble occasional words to each other. Sergeant Lloyd had seemingly taken a break from his interviews as he was sat, eyes closed and head back with a cigarette drooping from his lower lip. Mrs Corsewell had move to her usual table at the back of the room, sat at the table where Jean had first witnessed her. She sat as smartly dressed as ever, poised resting her chin on the back of her hand, which stood propped up by an elbow pressed into the soft white tablecloth, her eyes were firmly fixed downwards towards a book she had placed open in front of her. Mrs Corsewell's expression was still as serious as ever. Mrs Grey was stood with an equally as serious expression; she lent her back against the far wall of the dining room looking out towards the tables, much like a head mistress during school assemblies. The family with the two teenage boys all sat together around the same table as before, the two teenage boys were muttering quietly to themselves as their parents' browsed newspapers with crossed legs. A draft slowly swayed the drawn curtains behind Jean, the curtains were long, but hung just above the floor.

Jean shot up. Her eyes sprung open. A shrill and rattling scream burst from the kitchen. The room leapt from their casual positions.

The scream rang through the manor; Jean held her hands to her ears.

The scream was followed by the grating sounds of chairs shuddering backwards, as the guests, staff and Sergeant Lloyd made their way hastily behind the bar area and into the Kitchen.

Still with her palms pressed to her ears Jean shuffled after her mother who had followed suit, briskly walking behind the crowd. As Jean entered the kitchen, she caught sight of Mrs Well's balling up with glazed eyes and a horrified face. She was sat on the floor in front of the kitchen's metallic walk-in freezer door. The adults begun to console Mrs Wells while taking turns peering into the open freezer door, a piercing scattering of startled phrases and gasps sounded from the on looking crowd:

"Oh good lord."

"Hell!"

"No. No. No."

Some of the adults recoiled sharply from the door. Jean squeezed her way through the crowd of legs, placed one hand on the cold metal of the open door and twisted her head around to look inside the freezer.

The cold air hit her face and made its way into her lungs as she breathed in, she stared through the icy mist into the back of the freezer.

Inspector Lewis stood sagged and red in the corner of the freezer, his eyes glowered back at Jean's and his mouth hung agape, his hair was matted together in clumps, held fixed by frozen blood. A dim pale-yellow glow from the light of the freezer lit is distorted upright frame.

Jean felt her mother's hands grab her shoulders and quickly pull her away from the freezer entrance.

"It is not for you to see Jean." She said softly.

Abruptly the Room erupted with scared and angry statements.

"Another one."

"This is insane."

"He's just there, lifeless, morbid."

"No more, no more!"

Jean could make out the strained mumbles of Mrs Wells as she spoke up to Robert who was now stood beside her.

"What happens now, are we all waiting to end up murdered?"

A slightly queasy looking Robert attempted to offer some condolence: "I'm sure this is the last one Mrs Wells."

"There should not have been a first murder with two Police Officers present." Barked a scarlet faced Mrs Grey, she glared towards Sergeant Lloyd, with a few stray hairs escaping from her tightly pull back hair, Mrs Grey was not emitting the aura of control she once held over others when positioned behind her desk.

"Mrs Grey, It is now blindingly obvious to all that Mrs Moss was the first victim of murder!" Sergeant Lloyd bluntly spattered his statements at the direction of Mrs Grey, he stood tall and bulged his eyes.

"These more recent deaths appear far more gruesome, far more deliberate than an old lady falling downstairs." Mrs Corsewell interjected.

"I am quite amazed at the continued lack of respect and the repeated questioning of police practises. I shall remind you all that there is a murderer present in this Kitchen at this very moment who may wish to kill us all, some cooperation would be most welcome!" Sergeant Lloyd bellowed across the room.

After a few seconds of silence, the mother of the two teenage boys shouted over the heads of the mob still congregated in front of the freezer door.

"We have found a body in the kitchen, is it not sound reasoning to assume that it is the Cook?"

"Absolutely not!" Cook replied, she stood straight and loomed over the crowd with wily offended eyes.

"How dare you, I am innocent, any person could have placed a body in the freezer, it is never locked. Besides there are plenty more suspicious looking people within this room."

"Would you point out who you believe to look suspicious Ms Cook?" Sergeant Lloyd asked, jumping on the opportunity.

Feeling taken a back and slightly attacked Cook took a long step backwards out of the crowd, she extended a thin pointed finger out in front of her.

"Him for a start."

Collectively the crowd including Jean followed the direction of Cook's pointed accusation. Everyone stared at Mr Shean.

"Oi!" Mr Shean sharply sounded with surprise.

"He seems like a suspicious man, as he is a traveling TV salesman who dresses peculiarly." Cook explained.

In retaliation Mr Shean replied: "My occupation and the way I look do not make me a murderer. I would argue that having access to knives, rolling pins, weapons and a freezer big enough to store a body would make one appear far far far more likely to be a murderer!"

"I have been working all hours of the day, I have not had the time to commit murders." Cook sneered slightly with the delivery of her excuse.

"The murder of Mr Patel took place in a bathroom within a corridor that leads to your kitchen and my partner Inspector Lewis is currently a corpse in your freezer, both bodies are less than a minute walk away from where you have been throughout today, a minute is a very short period of time." Sergeant Lloyd stated as he glared stone-faced into the eyes of Cook.

Cook sighed angrily from her flared nostrils. "It was, not, me."

"We shall see. Now, everyone let us all walk back into the dining room, everyone is to stay seated in the room until further instructions, everyone keep an eye on each other. I shall make a few notes regarding the body of Inspector Lewis in the freezer, I shall join you all shortly."

Jean once again felt her mother's hands on her shoulders to guide her towards the bar exit of the kitchen. The crowd followed behind them.

18. A matter of extreme urgency

Jean looked down at the doily that framed her place mat concentrically, she gazed blankly at the intricate lace patterns, she did not imagine them to be the canopies of jungle trees, or even the lines of a complex treasure map, she simply noticed they were white, white like the bathroom tiles where the remains of Mr Patel still hung over a sink. The kitchen was also tiled white, with Mrs Wells and Cook's aprons being white and the ice of the freezer being white. She wondered how Inspector Lewis ended up within his cold coffin; she did not believe wolves would put bodies in a freezer and mentally confirm this to be an impossible hypothesis. She again dwelled on the thought of wolves she wondered if wolves would bite through flesh, and what marks would their teeth leave.

Sergeant Lloyd slapped the bar top fiercely and loudly to force everyone's attention towards him, he had emerged from the bar entrance to the Kitchen. Sergeant Lloyd roared across the room; Jean's head rose.

"Inspector Lewis has a considerable amount of mud frozen on to his shoes, before his unfortunate passing he had clearly been outside for a lengthy amount of time. Can I please ask you all to raise your hands if you yourself have been outside during the last twenty-four hours, or if you have seen another individual outside during this time frame."

All adults within the room obediently raised their arms.

"Right, I see then I shall ask you all to provide more information." Sergeant Lloyd paused, then looked towards the table where Jean and her mother were seated. "We shall begin at this side of the room and work our way backwards." He delivered a stern pointed finger towards Jean's mother.

"Ah, very well, I shall be just a moment Jean."

Jean watched her mother push back her chair, move a dark line of hair to one side of her glasses and take a seat a short distance away at the table where Sergeant Lloyd had been stationed. The Sergeant strode through the room to take his position opposite her. Jean was close enough to eavesdrop on their conversation.

"Your name Mrs?"

"My name is Ms Mary Maple."

"So please let me know who it is that you have seen outside within the last twenty-four hours, or why you yourself went outside within this time frame?" Sergeant Lloyd cut straight to the point. Jean's Mother drew a deep breath to begin her statement.

"I believe that this morning I witnessed one or two guests leave the Manor, as a result of the newspaper headlines, I also believe it is safe to assume that the Doorman of the Manor followed them outside. This afternoon both my daughter and I have stayed within the ground floor rooms of the building. Although I feel that you should know that during the period where you gave instructions to remain in rooms with multiple personnel present, I witnessed Robert, a member of Hill's Bottoms staff, making for the rear gardens of the manor unaccompanied." Sergeant Lloyd raised his eyebrows with intrigue as Jean's Mother paused for breath.

"My daughter and I believed this to be odd behaviour given the clear instructions you had delivered moments before, so we decided to follow him towards the courtyard. He had made his way up a ladder and was attempting to strike down a sack which had been caught on something high up on the Manor wall. When we questioned him on why he had chosen this particular moment in time to attempt to detach the bag, he replied that it needed to be removed as it had frightened Mrs Corsewell." Jean's Mother felt obliged to continue as Sergeant Lloyd had begun writing frantically within his black notebook.

"So, I have personally been outside, along with my daughter and I have witnessed Robert outside, along with one or two guests and the Doorman early this morning." Content with her detailed answer Jean's mother sat back in her chair and rearranged her crossed legs.

"Thank you very much Mrs Maple, thank you for the information, please take to your seat for the time being." Sergeant Lloyd said without lifting his head from the focus of his pages.

Jean's Mother pushed back her chair and strode over to Jean and gave her a rare smile. Jean was most interested to observe what was to happen next, her back was stretched tall and she sat forward on her chair.

"Robert, would you please come over." Ordered the Sergeant.

Robert, who was seated alone on the table alongside Jean and her mother's, shakily took to his feet before shuffling across the dining room. Visibly twitching he lowered himself slowly onto the dining chair in front of Sergeant Lloyd.

Sergeant Lloyd was equally as blunt with his first question as he had been with Jean's Mother.

"Who have you seen outside during the last twenty-four hours or why have you been outside during this time frame."

Roberts stammered into his response like an old car engine. "Well, well, I have seen a fair few people outside and I myself have been outside a number of times during the last twenty four hours."

"Yes, well then, please begin by listing who you have seen outside, and when." Dictated the Sergeant.

"Oh, Well, late last night, as I always do, I walked around the perimeter of the grounds to check for anything suspicious, or odd, but mainly to tidy up and to get some air. I always finish my walk with a short conversation with Mr Wardell who smokes a cigarette just outside the main entrance at just before eleven, which is often when I complete my walk of the perimeter." Robert took a long pause to think back over the last twenty-four hours, while Sergeant Lloyd watched him with impatient eyes.

"I, then, this morning, witnessed Mr Mastable and Miss Griffiths leave in haste, and Mr Wardell went outside also as he helped them with their bags." Robert scratched his head before proceeding.

"I have also seen Miss Maisy outside, as I have seen her through a window as she left on her way to the telephone box, and I believe she is the last person I have seen outside." As Robert feigned a smile.

Sergeant Lloyd loudly responded. "Are you not forgetting Mrs Maple and her daughter this afternoon?"

"Ah, yes I am terribly sorry, I also saw them this afternoon in the courtyard area." Robert had begun to nervously rub the outside of his leg and subtly rock back and forth on his chair.

After a drawn silent pause, to further add to Robert's air of unease, Sergeant Lloyd creaked forward to the edge of his chair, the room leaned in also.

"It is my understanding that you initially went outside to the courtyard alone, which went against my request for guests and staff to ensure that they were within a room occupied by at least one other person. So, can I ask, for what reason did you decide to go to the courtyard area alone?" Sergeant Lloyd asked slowly as he carefully considered his words.

Robert sat back, as if the wave of panic he felt had physically washed him backwards. He gave his jittery response:

"A grain sack, from god knows where, had become snagged on a wall of the manor. I grabbed a ladder and attempted to free the sack."

Sergeant Lloyd's stern expression did not waver.

"A caught grain sack, this certainly does not appear to me to be a matter of extreme urgency. Surely you must have realised that to go outside alone was to directly disobey my advice, and so would implicate you within a murder investigation. The snagged sack story is highly suspicious to say the least."

Robert's face shone crimson, the broken veins across his cheeks glowed and beads of sweat slithered down his brow. Robert placed his hands across the table and lent slowly towards Sergeant Lloyd, he moved in until his stomach pressed firmly against the table's edge. Sergeant Lloyd mimicked his actions, so that they both lent across the table.

With a hushed, raspy whisper Robert responded.

"I did not consider implicating myself at that moment in time; I was far more concerned that if I was to leave the sack, as it was, then Mrs Corsewell would be very upset."

After exhaling a bewildered groan Sergeant Lloyd reacted with a question.

"Why would Mrs Corsewell be upset, could you not have dealt with this small issue at a later time?"

"Well Officer, the sack blew in the wind and banged against Mrs Corsewell's window beneath, as I..."

"Now I understand." Interrupted Sergeant Lloyd as he begun to sport a smug grin.

"You are attempting to explain to me that you are more concern with following Mrs Corsewell's requests than the orders of a police officer. Why would you been more afraid of Mrs Corsewell than you would be of being implicated in a murder investigation?"

Robert gingerly spluttered his explanation. "Well, I would not say afraid, I just do not want to disappoint, and I wish to be seen as a good employee."

"Well Robert maybe it is commendable that you value your job so highly but giving the severity of murder I have to say it is an odd move to make."

"Sir, I swear to god that I have not been involved in any of these horrible events."

"May I ask whether or not you have strong alibies for the time periods where these murders likely took place?"

Although the questioning was most interesting to Jean she felt uncomfortable watching Robert becoming increasingly more nervous and agitated, she peered downwards, attempting to distract her eyes with the patterns of the carpet.

"Yes, yes, well I, I recall being at the fireplace when I heard the screaming of Mrs Moss and well, regarding Mr Patel, I was within room eleven fixing the window catch when I heard the noise caused within the hallway, as someone must have discovered his body."

Sergeant Lloyd sighed slightly and creaked forwards in his chair. "Robert, fixing a window catch also seems, to me, to be a fairly trivial task to attempt to complete, during a time where there has been a murder and a police officer has gone missing. Can any other individual back up the claims of your whereabouts during these events?"

Robert lent even further over the table closer to the Sergeant, he dipped his head and whispered words that were hardly audible. Jean closed her eyes in an attempt to hear Robert more clearly.

"I am scared of losing my job sir, it is often made apparent to me by both Mrs Grey and Mrs Corswell that I am now old and not as useful as perhaps I once was."

Sergeant Lloyd quickly moved back to rest against the back of his chair, he adopted a far more casual pose, and withdrew a pen from within the inside of his navy jacket. Robert sat frozen.

Jean's eyes open with the silence, the room awaited Sergeant Lloyds next words.

"Robert. Thank you for talking to me please return to your table."

19. *NO, NO, NO*

The members of the room sat facing the table occupied by Sergeant Lloyd, much like a jury awaiting the next witness to be summoned to the stands.

Jean enjoyed the drama that had unravelled, but she felt uneasy in knowing that the bodies of Mr Patel and Inspector Lewis remained within the manor. Jean also felt confined to her seat, it seemed inappropriate to move, or to make a sound, whilst the room remained fixated on the actions of Sergeant Lloyd. She wriggled tentatively to regain a more comfortable position, softly ruffling the bottom of her dress pressed between the backs of her legs and the chair.

Once his notetaking was complete Sergeant Lloyd rested back into his seat; the chair gave a creak that was oddly a welcome momentary interruption from the tedious sound of the ticks and tocks, which echoed from a clock placed within the entrance hallway.

Sergeant Lloyd inhaled deeply; the heads of the room rose in unison.

"Mr Shean, I do not believe that we have spoken enough, may I ask you some questions?" With his newly adopted seating arrangement Sergeant Lloyd appeared far more relaxed and composed.

A sheepish Mr Shean collected his bowler hat from the corner of his table and held it between his hip and elbow, with one hand he gripped a water glass and with the other a brown thick briefcase. He took long yet uneasy strides over to the Sergeant's table. He placed the briefcase to the left of the dining chair and the water glass on the table, as he took to his seat in an uncomfortable manor, poised with the straight back he sat as though he was within a job interview.

Sergeant Lloyd began. "I am aware, from looking through the Manor's guestbook that you are Mr Paul Shean, and that you are here on business, is any of this information incorrect?" Sergeant Lloyd asked somewhat rhetorically without leaving much of a pause, before quickly drawing breath for his next sentence. Mr Shean nervously interjected regardless.

"No, no, no Sir that is all correct."

"That is good, others seem quick to point the finger towards you, blaming you for the murders, do you understand why you could be considered as a suspect?" Sergeant Lloyd lowered his chin, pressing it firmly into his barrelled chest and narrowed his eyes to focus in on Mr Shean.

Rattled and taken aback by the question Mr Shean scratched his face and responded sharply, blurting out the words.

"I, no, no, no I cannot understand why, the hotel staff have not, they have not been particularly nice to me since my arrival."

Sergeant Lloyd moved his hand to his forehead and gripped his temples, as if the action would help to piece together his question.

"In what way do you believe they have been…. unsavoury towards you?"

Mr Shean's brow raised, the remaining few curls that jutted from the sides of his head bounced with the joy of having the opportunity to disparage the manor staff.

"Well now, it begun on a sour tone, once I had informed them that I was a television salesman it appeared that my stay was more of a hindrance to them than it was a service, which I was paying for. There are many down turned faces at this Manor, you are certainly not getting a smile out of any of them."

A low moan from a few of the manor staff brought Sergeant Lloyds attention away from Mr Shean, he looked around the room, and met eyes with Miss Maisy, who energetically rose from her post leaning nonchalantly on the bar and gave a beaming smile.

"Mr Shean I must say that I fully understand the point you are making regarding the odd attitudes of the manor staff, however if we put our small gripes aside for a moment, can you recall anything that you believe went a little further than just unsavoury behaviour?"

"Well of course, the Staff spoke openly about their feelings towards Mrs Moss, on multiple occasions I have overheard Mrs Grey speaking of her annoyance at Mrs Moss…"

"I am sorry, but I must interrupt!" Mrs Grey had stood up from her table, she continued. "These occasions that Mr Shean is referring to are conversations between myself and Mr Shean, where he also shared his opinions of annoyance towards Mrs Moss."

Mrs Grey paused, but as she had remained standing with a fierce scowl no one else felt it appropriate to speak, she once again continued.

"Mr Shean is a traveling T.V salesman, he is attempting to sell entertainment, may I propose that he does not appreciate the calming tranquillity of Hills Bottom Manor and took it upon himself to create his own entertainment." Mrs Grey barely drew breath. "He is also the youngest male within the manors walls and so appears to me to be the most capable of these murders."

Sergeant Lloyds eyebrows were raised, and his mouth drew a thoughtful expression across his face, he placed pen to paper.

A shudder of a chair pushed across carpeted floor shifted the rooms attention to the family with two boys placed in the corner. The Mother had stood up from her seat.

"May I also add that Mr Shean has been telling ghost stories to the children, which is extremely inappropriate given the current circumstances we find ourselves in!" Her raised voice echoed around the dining room and appeared to echo in the thoughts of Sergeant Lloyd as he momentarily hesitated during taking notes.

"NO, NO, NO, I have not told ghost stories to the children, Officer do not write that down." Mr Shean's face was both drawn and screwed in a way Jean had never seen a person's face to look.

Without moving or losing focus on her newspapers Jean's Mother calmly interposed:

"I can concur with the statement made by the Lady to my left."

Sergeant Lloyd placed his pen to the side of his black notebook spread open on the table in front of him; he sat up straight and met Mr Shean's peculiar gaze.

"Ghost stories?" He softly spoke with a disappointed tone.

"No not ghost, just a normal story and I only told Jane" Mr Shean gestured over to Jean.

Jean felt her face blush; she was most uncomfortable at being included within the adult's conversation.

"Her name is Jean." corrected Jeans Mother, again she spoke calmly without moving.

"Yes, Jean, I only told Jean a folk story a very normal story. These accusations only go to…"

"It was a story about dogs killing children!" shouted one of the boys from the corner family table.

The room collectively gasped. The gasp was immediately followed by the dull thud of the mother slapping a palm as hard as she could muster across the shoulder of the interrupting son.

Sergeant Lloyd drew breath and wrinkled his nose in disgust. "You told a story about dogs tearing apart children to a child?"

"It is the fable of Gelbert the Hound! It is a classic story!" Mr Shean's shirt had begun to develop dark patches where the fabric clung to his sweat; he sat fidgeting uncomfortably in his chair reacting to every word with increasingly distorted facial expressions.

Sergeant Lloyd seemingly ignored his explanation and continued his questioning.

"Mr Shean, I would like to note down your whereabouts during each of these three murders."

The room now had an equally as tense feel but the anger around the room appeared to have quelled, as both Mrs Grey and the mother of the corner family were now seated. Jean felt her eyes sting mildly; she suppressed a yawn by keeping her lips fixed together.

"Of Course, Officer, during Mrs Moss's fall I was asleep in my room."

"Do you believe that anyone saw you enter your room?"

"It is possible, but I did not notice anyone on the staircase as I made my way upwards. I was talking with Mrs Grey by the entrance desk when we heard of Mr Patel's death and I was with everyone as we took a look into the freezer to discover the other Officer."

There was a sombre silence as Mr Shean stopped after mentioning the discovery of Inspector Lewis's frozen end. The Sergeant continued to make notes for some time whilst Mr Shean sat nervously juddering.

"May I return to my table?" The sheepish question from Mr Shean reminded Jean of the girls from her old school who often spoke to teachers with a similarly uneasy tone.

Sergeant Lloyd flicked his hand out across the table, to which Mr Shean took as his signal to collect his bag and slowly make his way back to the comfort of his own table.

Sergeant Lloyd, without looking up from his notes, bluntly impatiently shouted to beckon the next individual for questioning.

"Cook!"

The shout jarred Jean's eyes a little wider; her eyelids were drifting downwards, resting slightly lower than normal.

"I shall not refer to you as Cook within my report, what is your name?"

The question had begun just as cook had made it over to the Sergeant's table, she grasped the top of the chair wrapping her long fingers around the back rest, she withdrew the chair forcefully from underneath the table and answered Sergeant Lloyd's question as she took to her seat.

"My name is Lily; you can refer to me as Lily"

"And your Surname?"

Cook looked upwards and rolled her eyes, Sergeant Lloyd gave an angry and exasperated exhaling of breath in her direction, as if to will the answer from her.

Cook crossed her arms tightly and leaned across the table.

"Corsewell." She sharply whispered.

Sergeant Lloyd's withstanding angry and exasperated demeanour did not waver as he repeated.

"Corsewell!" The room broke into a murmur.

Jean noticed the Manor staff exchanging perplexed looks.

"Well, that piece of information is something that I believe most people would have made apparent far more quickly than you have."

The confidence Cook had once exuded had lessened, her arms were crossed, her head lowered, and she spoke softer than before.

"I do not really know why it was anyone else's business, I am a Cook I am here to Cook."

"Well this is now my business, what other pieces of information are you hiding from the law?"

Cook gave lacklustre shrug. Sergeant Lloyd continued.

"What is your relation to Mrs Corsewell and why would you keep this to yourself?"

"I didn't think it would help matters for the other staff to know. That is to know that I am Mrs Corsewell's daughter"

"This conversation has already been extremely insightful Miss Corsewell." A grin grew across the round face of Sergeant Lloyd.

Jean's head became too heavy to bear, she placed one elbow onto the table and nestled her forehead into the crook, her eyes closed, with her fading consciousness she continued to eavesdrop on the conversation between Cook and Sergeant Lloyd.

"I am a Cook that is my role, I do not wish for people to know me personally. I have been in the Kitchen all working hours; I have nothing to do with the incidences."

"As Mrs Wells is the only other member of Kitchen staff, who currently still resigns within the Manor, can she back-up your claims of your whereabouts?" Both Sergeant Lloyd and Cook turned their head to face the bar where Mrs Wells leant.

"Myself and Mrs Wells are not joined at the hip, I do not know of her whereabouts at all times."

"Oi! Do not pull me down into this!" Yelled Mrs Wells from across the room, she had risen from her relaxed lean to now be stood as tall and as upright as her round body allowed her to appear.

Unfazed by Mrs Wells remarks Cook continued: "Officer if you are attempting to discover the individuals with the weakest alibies regarding their whereabouts then you have already found the most suspicious person." The room collectively held its breath as Cook paused.

"Robert! Robert is up and down the stairs, shuffling all over the place faffing on any task that he can draw out to last the entire day, his excuses relating to his whereabouts seemed uncertain even to him, I wouldn't be…."

"Robert…" Sergeant Lloyd raised his voice above Cook's. "Robert is an elderly man, I do not believe that he has the physical ability to cause such a horrible scene within the bathroom where Mr Patel is currently scattered, and I certainly do not believe he has the ability to murder Inspector Lewis and move his body into the freezer."

Robert sat mouth agape scarlet faced slumped at his table, frozen by the cutting words of both Sergeant Lloyd and Cook. Jean caught one final look through a squinted eye as she fell asleep.

20. *Traumatic events*

Jean awoke to a strong grip on her arm. Her Mother stood looming over her.

"Jean". Her Mother's exclamation was impatient, she gave an upwards nod, which Jean took as a signal to raise her head up off the table. As her eyes adapted to the dim lighting of the dining room she wriggled from her seat and stood, with shoulders and eyes lids slump, by her mother's side.

All guests and staff stood behind their tables, Sergeant Lloyd begun a slow walk towards the entrance hall, after some hesitation Jean and her mother followed suit along with the other members of the dining room.

"You shall all be safe; I shall keep an eye on every corner of this Manor."

Sergeant Lloyd swung his arms in a gleeful manor to beckon others to following him down the hall; the gleeful swinging of arms did not hide the apprehensive atmosphere.

Jean could hear the soft muttered comments of guests and staff as they all trudged further down the entrance hall to the foot of the staircase.

"I will not sleep a wink"

"Safe?……safe?….."

"The cheek."

Jean turned her head as she walked by her mother's side, Sergeant Lloyd looked up at her from the foot of the staircase, he watched as the inhabitants of the manor ascended upwards towards their rooms.

The staircase was a particular struggle for Jean, she could feel the weight of her shoes, it was a welcomed accomplishment to see her warped reflection within the golden 49 metal room number dozily gazing back at her.

"Clean up Jean." Her Mother instructed as they entered.

Without cognition Jean moved herself and her heavy shoes into the room's bathroom.

As she closed the door behind her she once again caught sight of her dozy gaze in the long bathroom mirror above the sink. She autonomously changed into a long mauve sleeping gown, grabbed a toothbrush and squeezed a thick ribbon of striped toothpaste across the bristles. Her hand regimentally moved back and forth in front of her lips, whilst her eyes wearily wondered around the bathroom. She inspected each white tile fastidiously, she thought back to the mauled state of Mr Patel, if something similar had happened within this bathroom then maybe there would be a missed speck of blood, she thought to herself. Besides miss-coloured grouting there were no abnormalities.

Jean twisted the brass nob of the bathroom door to stagger and writhe herself underneath the covers of her window side bed. The moonlight briefly cast a strip of white light across her pillow, as it momentarily shone through a break in the night clouds. Despite the thoughts of the day's traumatic events lingering in Jean's mind she fell asleep.

21. Cries of disorientation and despair

Jean awoke to the sharp click of metal striking metal. She rose swiftly to peer across the room at her mother fastening the metal latches of her travel case.

"I'm glad that you are awake Jean, I think that we ought to leave."

Jean's mother took a large step across the room, she gently tapped her palm on an outfit that had been placed at the foot of Jean's bed.

Understanding her mother's instructions Jean slipped from the bed and collected the items of clothing on her way towards the bathroom. Whilst changing, Jean once again inspected the white tiles, the grouting lines which framed them seemed darker than before. Her mother's impatient rap on the door quickened Jean's pace as she slid on her blue buckled loafers.

Jean's Mother stood with two bags held within one hand, the other gripping the handle of the room's door. As Jean made eye contact with her she swung the door open to reveal the noise of the stairwell.

Jean could hear the sound of footsteps running and an abundancy of raised voices. The sounds echoed up from the entrance hallway.

The pair scuttled down the worn carpet of the stair sets, for the last time they passed the landing where a portrait of an elderly man dressed in black had overseen the death of Mrs Moss. As Jean took to the last step she looked down the entrance hall, towards a handful of people who made up a crowd around Mrs Grey's desk.

The Manor's large Entrance doors swung open fiercely, both leaves and Mr Wardell blew in, followed by a tall lanky figure dressed in a tan trench coat.

The crowd turned to face the Manors newest visitor.

"I am Chief Constable Nobel move aside!" Constable Nobel's croaky shouted words echoed through the Manor.

"Bloody Hell!" His eyes darted violently around the hall as the crowd continued to step away from him.

Jean and her mother joined the back of the gathering. Jean now had sight of the entrance desk where the crowd were once gathered.

Gaunt and grey led a lifeless Robert, spread across the entrance desk, with his head hanging off one edge, his haunting motionless eyes stared back at Jean's. Thick lines of blood drawn from his chest had made their way across his face and into his matted hair, his green blazer hung torn from the side of the desk.

Jean gasped softly.

"For God's sake, get the child out of here!" barked Constable Nobel.

Jean's Mother bent over to meet Jean's eyes. "Why don't you wait over here for a short while Jean."

Jean's Mother softly pushed her in the lounge area and placed their two cases beside her.

No one occupied the lounge; Jean stood next to the green chairs and gazed momentarily at the black lifeless fireplace. Although her eyes wandered around the room she could only see the red streaked face of Robert in her mind.

After her shock subsided, she noticed the chess board, another piece had joined the other toppled three. She slowly stepped closer to inspect. The jade fourth sideways piece reminded Jean of a tulip flower, a tulip flower which held a ball on top of its closed petals; it was an elegant and tall piece.

She turned back to witness her mother squeezed amongst the gathering beside Robert's flaunted cadaver. Jean enjoyed the serenity of the empty lounge, it was of stark contrast to the angry tone of the crowded entrance hall, she watched through the frame of the lounge archway.

Jean felt it appropriate to stand all fallen chess pieces back to their upright orientation, but as she was unsure of where they should be placed on the checkerboard, she decided that they should create their own line independent from the others. As she placed the pieces softly down onto the dark wood of the table top she wondered what the aim of the game was, she looked closely at each piece and then at the white and black squares of the board, she deduced that Chess might be a pattern creation game, with the players mission being to complete a certain pattern made from the colours of the pieces and the black and white squares, perhaps the height of each piece denotes where within the pattern it should be placed.

Jean flinched. Her mother's hand grabbed her shoulder tightly.

"It is time Jean, let's go!" Her mother met Jean's eyes with the briefest of intense stares, before she began a pacey stride, dragging Jean along with her. Jean's legs moved quicker than was comfortable as she struggled to keep up.

Her mother seized the two cases with one hand and the pair made their way back into the entrance Hall. The crowd's tone had escalated to beyond angry; the hallway had descended into a shouting scrum of fuming faces.

"How dare you! How dare you!" Screamed Mrs Corsewell as Constable Nobel pulled her arm towards himself, handcuffs at the ready.

"I told you so! What horrid creatures!" Shouted Mr Shean as he stretched his neck above the crowd.

Jean and her mother squeezed past the corner family, the mother held her two boys tightly to her hip.

The entrance door was open with Mr Wardell standing off to one side. Jean caught the eye of Mr Wardell as the chilled morning breeze shivered the back of her neck, Mr Wardell stared back frozen, bemused.

Mr Wardell creaked the teak brown monolithic set of doors closed behind Jean and her mother, Jean took one final look behind her, through the slither of the doorway she caught sight of a puzzled Sergeant Lloyd with his head fixated on his black notebook.

"My book. This is not my book! None of my notes are in here!" His echoed cries of disorientation and despair were silenced as the door clanged shut.

Jean's Mothers pace had not slowed, the pair's shoes harshly crunched the gravel as they strode across the courtyard towards the road in front of the manor.

An elderly gentleman dressed in a long black coat and flat cap was stood on the road.

"Mrs Maple?" He asked.

"Yes, yes, yes." Replied Jean's mother.

The elderly man lunged across the road toward a parked taxi, opened the back door. Jean slid inside followed at first by the two cases and then her mother.

"Thank you!" Jean's mother yelled in a fluster as the taxi pulled away.

Looking past both cases and her mother Jean caught a final glimpse of Hills Bottom Manor.

Jeans mother softly sighed with exasperation, before leaning over the cases to look at Jean through her round glasses, which held up a straight cut fringe.

"Jean, I noticed that you liked the chess board, chess is an excellent game, I shall teach you the rules soon, but, how about for our next game I shall play Mrs Green and you shall be Miss Gillian Green. Maple was a little too quaint for us anyway. I'm sure the next hotel shall be far more interesting. How do you like the sound of that Gillian?"

Gillian nodded with a smile at the thought of another adventure, she was quite happy with the name Gillian Green. She turned away from her mother and looked at the raindrops which had begun to rest on the car window.

Raindrops on car windows can be anything.

End

Printed in Great Britain
by Amazon